LETTERS TO MY DAUGHTER'S KILLER

Cath Staincliffe

Constable & Robinson Ltd
55–56 Russell Square
London WC1B 4HP
www.constablerobinson.com

First published in the UK by C&R Crime,
an imprint of Constable & Robinson Ltd., 2014

ISBN 978-1-78033-570-4 (hardback)
ISBN 978-1-47211-730-4 (Trade paperback)
ISBN 978-1-78033-572-8 (ebook)

Typeset by TW Typesetting, Plymouth, Devon

Pri⋯⋯⋯⋯⋯⋯⋯⋯⋯⋯⋯⋯⋯⋯⋯⋯ 4YY

ACKNOWLEDGEMENTS

Two publications provided me with invaluable research: *Review into the Needs of Families Bereaved by Homicide* by Louise Casey CB and *Guiding Children Through Trauma and Grief* by Jean Harris-Hendriks, Dora Black and Tony Kaplan (I'm leaving out the full book title here to avoid spoilers). A big thank you to Anne Graham who shared her experiences of working in libraries. And a cheer for librarians everywhere. Many thanks go to Krystyna Green and the team at C&R Crime and to my agent Sara Menguc for unstinting and generous support, encouragement and enthusiasm. I'm very grateful to Mary Sharratt and Kath Pilsbury for feedback on my work in progress – and for laughs along the way. Finally a big thanks (again) to Tim for everything – I couldn't have done it without you.

For my wonderful dad
David Staincliffe 1930–2013
Just the love

Part One

CHAPTER ONE

17 Brinks Avenue
Manchester
M19 6FX

I hate you. My first letter, and that is all I want to say. I hate you. But those three words can barely convey the depth, the breadth, the soaring height of this hatred. Nearly four years, and what has taken me by surprise is that these feelings, of rage and the desire for vengeance, have not diminished but have grown. Time has not healed them but stoked the fires. The hatred has been forged into something steely, into a rock so dense and heavy inside that I fear it is killing me too. Crushing me. Taking what is left of my life and leaching the goodness, the joy, the optimism from it. So I am writing to you in the vain hope, for I think it is vain, that some communication can help me move beyond or around this pit of hate.

With each passing month the monster grows stronger. I lie awake at night imagining all the many and lurid ways I could hurt you. Longing to punish you, to make you scream and beg for release. My head full of scenarios from Jacobean trage-dies: hot pokers and the rack. From black prison ops: rendition flights and redacted statements, naked men in hoods, men with pliers, electricity cables and water. From serial killer stories: the blade in the eyes or between the legs, messages daubed on walls in blood.

Your violence has bred this violence in me, a cuckoo child that would devour me, from the inside out.

This is no way to live.

You won't be replying to me. We're not pen pals. The only way I'll countenance contact with you at all is if I set the parameters. So you will read my letters. No salutation, you'll note, no *Dear* or *Sir*; that sticks in my craw. I have a lot to tell you, a lot you need to know, to understand. It's all at my fingertips. I kept a journal, you see, put it all in there, an attempt to make sense of things, navigate the nightmare. Impressions, thoughts, notes of everything I wanted to say to you. So, I will send those letters, and then when I am ready, you will answer my questions. They began that night almost four years ago, and like the hatred they have grown and multiplied. So much I still do not know. Because you denied the crime, contested the charge, because you lied and lied and lied. Two questions haunt me most: *Why did you kill her?* And *How did she die?*

I doubt whether you have the slightest inkling of what it's been like for me. Too busy saving your own skin. So I am going to tell you. You will hear it in full, no interruptions, no arguments. The whole of it: 3D, with director's commentary and extra scenes.

Brace yourself.

Ruth

CHAPTER TWO

17 Brinks Avenue
Manchester
M19 6FX

It starts with a phone call. Or should I say it ends there? Because that is the point of no return. The moment my world slips on its axis.

That fine September evening, 2009, I am home alone as usual. My latest short-term lodger has returned to London and I've no one else booked in. I was out the night before with my friend Bea, to the cinema. *District 9*, the thriller about aliens and prejudice in South Africa. My Saturday unrolls with a comforting routine: a lie-in until nine (the best I can muster with my advancing age – I am fifty-seven), a trip to the newsagent for the weekend *Guardian* and a slow breakfast reading it, my cat Milky curled on my lap.

A walk to the village for fish. It's not been a village in that isolated, hamlet sort of way for decades, but we do that here: Levenshulme village, Withington, Didsbury, Chorlton. Perhaps because the joining-up of all the villages to form the city is relatively recent. A couple of hundred years ago and 'the village' was a handful of farms and a toll road. Now it's just another neighbourhood in Manchester, Britain's second city.

I'm not working at the library today: I do every other Saturday, but it's my weekend off. After some chores – washing

5

sheets and hanging them out to dry, emptying the litter tray, cleaning the sink – I eat lunch, then go up to the allotment. We've had it for years; officially the tenants are Frank and Jan, but when they first got hold of it, they invited Melissa and Mags and Tony and me to join in. It felt less overwhelming than tackling it on their own, as it was completely overgrown, a wilderness of dock leaves and brambles and dandelions. The division of labour between six of us worked well on the whole, especially as crises occurred every so often, affecting people's availability. Then last year Frank and Jan moved to Cornwall and Tony and I had been divorced for years, so we were down to three. Neither of the others are here this afternoon, though I can see from the state of the beds that they've harvested some potatoes recently.

The sun is warm, warm enough for me to shed my jumper once I start digging. This time of year the plot is full of produce, and after I've knocked the bulk of the dirt off the potatoes and cleared up any tubers I can find, I collect some leeks and runner beans, carrots and salad stuff: lettuce and radishes and some tomatoes from the greenhouse. There are other allotment-holders working their plots, and we stop to chat in between our efforts.

After a couple of hours my back is protesting. I do some watering, then clean the tools and lock them in the shed. My little harvest will feed me through the week, and I pick some bunches of sweet peas and chrysanthemums to brighten up the house.

Milky goes crazy as I grill the mackerel, and he gets the fish skin for his pains. A soak in the bath with my book marks the start of my evening; a habit left over from the early years of bathing Lizzie when she was little, then topping up the water for myself.

As I'm sitting down to watch television, Lizzie texts me asking if I can babysit Florence the following Saturday; she'll

6

let me know what time when she's checked with Jack, who's out at the gym. Glad to be asked, I agree immediately.

I'm brushing my teeth, getting ready for bed, looking forward to fresh sheets, when the phone rings.

I almost don't answer. Some childish part of me likes to imagine that things might have been different if I'd ignored the ringing. But they wouldn't. Even with another half-hour of blissful ignorance.

I had no premonition, no sudden goose bumps, no telepathic sensation that things were wrong during the evening. Shouldn't I have sensed that Lizzie was in danger, that she was fighting for her life? That she was losing. People talk of knowing, of pain in the heart or sudden waves of dread, of dreams and waking nightmares, of a sudden overpowering urge to talk to someone or get home. Animal instincts.

Nothing for me, no alarm bells, no early-warning system. When I answer the phone, I'm calm, relaxed, sleepy.

'Hello?' I say, and it's Jack, my son-in-law, his voice almost unrecognizable.

'Ruth. Oh God, Ruth.' Then comes the first rush of fear, pepper-shot on my skin, a twist to my guts. But it is little Florence, my granddaughter, I fear for. An accident, a sudden death, blue-lipped in her small bed.

'Jack?' It's a question. An invitation. *Tell me* is what I'm saying.

And he does. 'It's Lizzie. Oh Ruth, someone's hurt Lizzie. Oh God.'

I am grappling to make sense of his words. My heart is beating in my throat. 'Is she all right?' I say. I know she's not. I can hear it in the way his breath comes so rapidly and I know that if she was all right he'd have said that first. Still, we are hardwired to hope.

'I think they've killed her.' He is crying.

Killed! 'Call the police,' I say. I think of this instead of what

7

he's told me. I don't want to think about that. I cannot. It's not possible, it can't be true. I set it aside as too much to handle. Preposterous anyway. Easier to focus on something else. 'Call the police,' I repeat.

'I have, they're coming.'

My thoughts won't be stifled. They rear up shrieking in my mind. *Killed!* Broderick Litton. Lizzie's stalker. He's obsessed with her. The police never did anything, not even when he turned up at her house. All they said was they would talk to him. Stalking wasn't a crime back then. He frightened her; he was a big man, over six feet tall, and soft-spoken. He sent her gifts and watched her performances. At first she thought it was funny but a bit sad. It quickly became oppressive. Then scary. She carried pepper spray and a personal alarm. He threatened her at the end, wrote letters saying she'd be sorry, he'd make her pay. Lizzie took them to the police. Then it all went quiet. Over a year since she's heard anything, so long enough for her to relax again, to lower her guard. And now this. Oh God, we should have been vigilant. We should have insisted. Echoes bang in my head, other stories, other people's daughters, inquiries into police negligence, failure to act, ensuing tragedies. All the cases where harassment turned to murder. We didn't do enough, and now this.

'Broderick Litton,' I say to Jack.

'I'll tell them,' he says.

'Where are you? At home?'

'Yes.'

'Florence?'

'She's fine. She was fast asleep.'

'I'll be there in a minute.'

I'm still dressed, so it's a matter of moments to get my car keys and pull on shoes. It's not far to Jack and Lizzie's, a ten-minute walk, a two-minute drive. I arrive just before the ambulance. I see it coming from the other direction and it turns

8

in to Lizzie's street seconds after I do. An ambulance gives me faith. They will save her, they can do all sorts these days. There are bubbles in my chest, hysteria.

In my hurry to get out of the car, I trip and fall, scramble up. Jack is at the gate, Florence in his arms. His expression is drawn, harrowed in the street light. His teeth are chattering. The little girl has her face buried in his neck. I clutch his arm and he leans in towards me. When I stroke Florence's head, she shrugs me off, her narrow shoulders moving under her pyjamas.

Edging past them, I run up the path to the door and Jack calls my name. There's a whooping sound cut short as a police car pulls up near the ambulance. Blue lights flash around the cul-de-sac.

The door is half open. I push it wide and step inside. The lights are on in the kitchen-diner to my left and the living room area. All open-plan. An advertising jingle prattles from the TV. Lizzie is on the floor. I cannot see her face, it is hidden by her hair. Her blonde hair is drenched in blood. There is blood on her clothes, her camisole vest and cotton trousers, the sort of thing she wears to sleep in, more blood on the wooden floor. Firelight flickers on her arm, her hand.

I turn cold, wild panic sizzling through me. My heart contracts. Blood thrums in my ears. 'Lizzie,' I call to her, move forward, wanting to clear the hair from her face, help her up, help her breathe, but hands are pulling me back, people shouting, dragging me away, pushing me outside. I resist, try to fight them off, desperate to see my girl, but they hold me tighter, instruct me to do as I'm told, to let them do their job.

We are moved, Jack and Florence and I, taken further down the street. Various people ask questions. I feel like batting them away, my eyes locked on the doorway, waiting for them to bring Lizzie out and put her in the ambulance, get her to hospital. My frustration is so great that I round on the next person who comes to us. 'Why aren't they taking her to hospital?'

'Mrs Sutton?' he checks. 'Lizzie's mother?'

'Yes,' I snap.

His face softens with pity and my throat closes over.

'I'm sorry, Mrs Sutton, Lizzie is dead. We're treating it as suspected murder. The Home Office pathologist is on his way and the area will be cordoned off for our forensic teams to start their work. Would you be able to take Florence home with you?'

My mouth clamped tightly shut, I nod my head.

'Mr Tennyson – Jack – will be giving us a statement. And we'll want to talk to you later. There will be a family liaison officer to help you. They've been alerted. I am very sorry,' he says, 'but I need to ask you a few questions now, in case there's anything that might help us. You went in the house?'

'Yes.'

'Did you use a key?'

'The door was open,' I say.

'Unlocked, you mean?'

'No . . . erm . . . yes. It wasn't pulled shut.'

He writes down what I tell him. 'Where did you go?' he says.

'Just inside the living room.'

'Did you touch the front door?'

I think back. 'Yes, I pushed it.'

'Did you touch Lizzie?'

'No.' I didn't get the chance. I wish I had.

'Did you touch anything else?'

'No.'

'Think, anything at all: to steady yourself, perhaps? Or did you pick anything up?'

'I can't remember. I don't think so.'

He writes some more, then says, 'Because you've entered the crime scene, we need to take your clothes and your shoes. How close do you live?'

I tell him.

'We'll send someone with you now; if you can change immediately and put everything you're wearing in the bags you're given.'

'Broderick Litton,' I say, 'he stalked Lizzie. She reported it. You lot did nothing. You must find him.' I'm shivering, my words broken up. My knees buckle. He reaches out an arm and steadies me.

'Do you have an address, date of birth?' he says.

'No. Check your files – there must be something there.'

'We will do.' But he goes nowhere. 'We'll take further details when someone comes round to you – they won't be long.'

Jack brings Florence to the car. She's fallen asleep and barely stirs when he eases her into the booster seat I keep in the back.

'What happened?' I ask him before we part.

'I don't know,' he says, shaking his head, fresh tears streaking down his face. 'I'd been to the gym. She was fine when I left. I just saw her . . .' He can't go on, and I hold him close. One of the police officers gets in the passenger seat and I start the engine.

Florence has a little bed in my room for when she comes to stay, but I'm not going to sleep and I don't want her to wake up alone after all this. Did she see Lizzie? Did Jack manage to get her downstairs and out of the house without her waking? He'd have had to walk through the living room with her. The house is small, modern, the only thing they could afford.

Oh God. Jack was at the gym, so Florence must have been in the house when . . .

I lay Florence on the sofa and cover her with a blanket.

I change out of my jumper and jeans and walking shoes and put them into separate bags, and the policeman takes them away.

The house is cold, so I go into the kitchen and put the heating on. Milky comes and weaves around my legs. I stare at the vegetables on the counter, the crumbs of soil drying on them, the wispy roots of the carrots, the vivid green of the runner bean pods. Out of the window is a black sky and a frail new moon, scimitar-bright.

My head aches, a thudding pain beating in my temples and behind my eyes, and the words *Lizzie's dead* go round and round to the beat of that drum. But they are just words. I can't believe them. Not when I look at the carrots and the slice of moon and the child at peace on my sofa.

Ruth

CHAPTER THREE

17 Brinks Avenue
Manchester
M19 6FX

Did you think you'd got away with it, that first night? What were you feeling? Elation? Terror? Some sexual frisson? It's the same physiological response, isn't it – fight, flight, fuck. Violence, fear, sex. It's on my list of questions. And did you replay events in your head or try to shut them out? Were you racked with guilt or full of exhilaration?

While I wait for someone to come, to break the spell, me and my granddaughter and the cat cocooned in the bubble, I try to imagine you. Broderick Litton, who I never met, never saw. Like a bodyguard, Lizzie said you were; smart, though, a military type, clipped and polished. Always very pleasant except when you were being a vicious bully. At the time you were stalking her, I grew more panicky than Lizzie. When the police did so little, I wanted her to move. Suggested we swap houses.

The questions swoop through my head like bats in the dark, to and fro, silent, quick and shadowy. Why wasn't Lizzie more careful? Why did she open the door? Why did she let you in? Why? Why? Why?

Where are you? Scurrying through night-black streets smelling of blood, or lurking in some lair, drinking and gloating, or slipping into bed beside your drowsy wife?

It is hard to sit still and Milky senses my agitation, echoes it with repeated sorties out of the cat flap and back. My skin is cold; I am frozen to the marrow, despite the heating being on, and I'm itchy. I can't stop scratching: my arms, my neck, my calves. As if I am shedding a skin, or trying to claw it off and make my body raw like the rest of me.

Lizzie's photographs – Lizzie as a baby, as a child, with Jack, with Florence – clutter my walls. I am standing in the corner, staring at one: her graduation day, Lizzie flanked by Tony and me. Her eyes alive with happiness, ours too. Delight and pride. I rub at my shoulder. Tony – I must ring Tony. Should I? Or wait? Make completely sure? If there's been a horrible mistake and I tell him now . . . that she is . . . A wave of nausea breaks through me, coating me in clammy sweat, shrivelling my stomach, forcing bile into the back of my throat. In the kitchen I spit it out and drink a little water.

A knocking at the door makes me jump. It is the family liaison officer. A beanpole of a woman with short greying hair and a weather-beaten face. Kind eyes. Stupid thing to say really, but they are not brash or judgemental, or even overtly emotional, but accepting. The sort of eyes you can stare into and not feel impelled to look away. (Or maybe that's hindsight. Those early days, Kay, that was her name, was a sort of calm anchor for us all.)

Kay makes tea and explains what is happening, what will happen in the next twenty-four hours. That is as much as I can take in, and even that doesn't really penetrate. There is a buffer between my understanding and the outside world, a fog that makes it hard to truly hear and know things.

'It's the shock,' Kay says, when I apologize and ask her to repeat something. 'You won't be able to think straight,' she says. 'It's normal.'

A flare of anger pierces the fug. I take issue. 'This is not normal, none of this is normal.'

'No,' she agrees.

I pace the room; my scalp itches, I rake at it with my nails. And I try to remember what Kay has said. People will be busy at Lizzie's house documenting the scene and collecting evidence. There will be a post-mortem. A host of television dramas come to mind, angst-ridden pathologists and flawed but courageous detectives. This is real, I tell myself. Real. Really happening. There will be the formal identification of Lizzie's body. Kay says that, 'Lizzie's body', not 'the body'. Every time she mentions her, she uses Lizzie's name. Keeping it specific and personal. They are probably trained to do that. I appreciate it. The understanding that their victim is more than a victim; she's my daughter, Jack's wife, Florence's mother.

'I should ring Tony,' I remember in a rush. 'Lizzie's dad.'

'Does he live nearby?'

'Reddish Vale.' A few miles. 'He remarried,' I say, 'Denise.'

Denise the wheeze. My nasty nickname because Denise's default position is to giggle, to laugh, and she is a smoker, which adds to the breathy quality of her chortling. It's probably a nervous tic, but it makes me want to slap her. Grab her by the arms and ask her what's so funny.

I have to look their number up in my address book; it's not something I ever wanted to memorize. It rings and rings. Tony probably can't hear it. He's going deaf, Lizzie said recently, but he's too proud or too macho to get his ears tested. Lizzie teased him about it, and said she'd have to teach him sign language. A bit more than the few signs we mastered when she first began learning BSL: hello, goodbye, I love you and a couple of swear words. She brings me titbits about Tony (and no doubt does the same in the other direction), and I accept them gracefully. We keep it civilized. For her as much as anything. And for Florence.

The phone rings out. 'They're not answering,' I say to Kay. 'I'll try his mobile.'

Tony uses it for work but switches it off when he is at home. Or he used to. It seems to take forever to find my phone and his details. While it rings, it occurs to me that the Tennysons, Jack's parents, need to know too. I mention it to Kay. 'Should I wait?' Have I even got their number?

'Jack will probably want to tell them himself,' Kay says.

'Of course.'

She knows the etiquette, not just of death but of this particular situation: sudden, violent death.

Tony's cell phone goes to voicemail and I hang up. Bury my head in my hands.

'Try again in a while,' Kay says. 'Or we can send someone round there if you—'

'No.' It seems cowardly to do that. I should be the one to tell him, not some stranger.

The man who comes to take my statement seems far too young to be dealing with this sort of thing. But he's not at all nervous or inept. He takes me slowly through the sequence of events: Jack's call, the car journey, going into the house, being restrained.

Then he asks more questions about the house. Were the lights on or off, did I put any lights on? Was there any sound, TV or radio? What was the temperature like?

I laugh at this; it seems preposterous that in the face of such a huge shock, my sense of hot and cold would be functioning and that I might still remember.

'No idea,' I say.

I picture Lizzie, the contrast of her hair and the dark stains. Recall light flickering over her hand, her left hand. That would have been from the fire, their log-burning stove. 'The fire was lit,' I say.

Then the questions become more general, he confirms Lizzie's date of birth and age. He wants to know about her life, her work, her marriage, her routines. When I last saw her. What we spoke about. And finally if I can think of anyone who

16

might have wanted to cause her harm. I tell him all I can about Broderick Litton, urge him to check the police files. Surely they will know more than me.

He writes it all up and reads it back to me. Four pages in all. And I sign in the proper place.

When I call Tony again, Denise answers.

'It's Ruth, I need to talk to Tony.'

There's a wait while she fetches him or takes him the phone, and then his voice, thick with sleep. I say his name and then I freeze. I swallow. Force breath into my lungs. 'Tony, I've got some really, really bad news. Oh Tony. It's Lizzie. I'm so sorry. Lizzie, she's dead.'

He makes a noise, a sort of howl, strangulated.

I can't tell him the rest, not on the phone. 'Can you come?'

'Yes,' he says. That's all he says. Just yes. Quick and quiet. And hangs up.

Jack gets back first; it is almost dawn. His eyes are red, his lips chapped, his face grey. He is wearing navy jog pants and black trainers and a nylon anorak which the police must have given him to replace his clothes. He takes the coat off, moving slowly like an arthritic old man, and sits beside Florence, still sleeping on the sofa.

There's no mistaking whose daughter she is. The same shiny straight black hair and even features, prominent cheekbones. The only thing Florence got from Lizzie are her eyes, sea green, the same as Tony's.

Jack's been the main carer the last couple of years. Lizzie and he are both freelance, so whoever has work offered grabs it and the other person picks up the domestic reins. It's hard for them – juggling, coping with the uncertainty of money – but they both love their work and neither of them would swap it for the security of doing something tedious nine to five.

17

Jack will do anything he can get: radio parts, panto, telly, as well as theatre, which he likes best. He keeps going up for auditions but hasn't had anything for months, whereas Lizzie's been flat out. She first began interpreting at conferences and for deaf students at the universities here, then developed her theatre work, which has really taken off.

Kay brings Jack a cup of tea and he wraps his hands around it and hunches over. She tells him what she's already told me about the day ahead. About what will happen to Lizzie. What must be done. She leaves us to talk.

He is clearly exhausted, but I am desperate to know what he saw, to hear the sequence of events, to find out if he's learnt anything yet from the police.

'What happened?' I ask him.

He shakes his head. 'They don't know.' His voice is worn out, husky, almost gone. 'I'd been to the gym . . .' He tries to clear his throat. 'She was watching TV when I left . . .'

They both go to the gym regularly. Lizzie likes it as a way of keeping fit, and Jack has to keep in shape for his work in the theatre.

'I got back . . .' His hands tighten round the mug. 'She was there . . .' his composure breaks and he speaks, fighting tears, 'she was there, like that. Who could do that?' He looks at me.

'Did you see anyone?'

Jack shakes his head, ruination in his eyes.

'Broderick Litton,' I say.

'They know. They'll interview him.'

'She's not had any trouble from him recently?'

'No, nothing since last July.'

'And she'd never have let him in,' I point out.

'She might have thought it was me, that I'd forgotten something,' Jack says.

'You'd use your key.'

18

'Forgotten that, then – I don't know.' He casts about. 'We had a prowler.'

'What? When?'

'Wednesday night. There'd been a break-in at number eight on Tuesday.' Two doors down. 'Lizzie saw someone in our back garden.'

'Was it Litton?'

'She said not, not tall enough, more like a kid, she thought, though she didn't see his face,' Jack says. 'The police came round on the Thursday morning – I told them then.'

'Have they caught him?'

'We never heard anything.'

I rub my forehead. Could it be this prowler and not Litton?

'They always look at the husband, don't they?' he says.

My stomach turns over. 'They have to. They can't possibly think . . .' Shock stings around my wrists.

'No,' he says, 'they know I wasn't there. But having to go over it and over it. I tried to wake her . . .' He puts the mug on the floor, covers his face, shoulders shaking.

I go to him, sit on the arm of the sofa and hug him tight.

Light steals into the room, hurting my eyes.

Kay comes back; she hasn't slept either. Is she used to it – all-nighters for work?

'Did they say how she died?' I ask Jack. I know there was blood. Too much blood.

'They said the post-mortem would confirm it.' Jack's mouth trembles as he speaks. 'Blunt trauma?' He looks at Kay, as if checking he's said it correctly.

'Blunt force trauma,' she says. 'That's what we think at the moment.'

'With what?' I can't imagine.

Did you bring a weapon with you? A baseball bat or a cosh of some sort? Then it occurs to me that perhaps you used your

19

fists. That feels worse. Was it the first time you'd killed someone? And why pick Lizzie? What did you come to the house for? Money? To steal? To rape? How did you get in?

I go outside for air, out the back. The garden glitters with dew, spiderwebs and lines hang on the shrubs around the border. The air is damp and cool and my windpipe hurts as I draw some in. A pair of coal tits are on the peanut feeder in the magnolia tree. The sky is blue, blushing pink in the east. That slice of moon still visible. Milky stalks out and sits under the tree. The tits ignore him. How can it all be here, just so? It all feels too bright and clear, too high-definition, as though I've wandered on to a film set.

On the roof of the terraced row at the back, three magpies bounce and chatter. A crow joins them, edging along to the chimney, then another. And two more. *A murder of crows.* The phrase springs unbidden, a booby trap, like some ghastly practical joke my mind plays on me.

I'm aware of commotion from inside. Then Tony is here, coming out of the patio door, and Denise behind him. Tony is shaking his head as he reaches me; he embraces me, a hard, swift pressure before he steps back. And it's all I can bear. Resisting the sense memory of a thousand other hugs, his height, his bulk a comfort. Before I know it I'm hugging Denise, who's not laughing now. We've never touched before, not even a handshake.

We're a similar height, Denise and I. Both with that padding that comes with middle age. Even if my arms and legs retain their original shape, my belly sticks out and my bum seems to have doubled in size. Denise is chunkier than me, fatter in the face too. She smells of perfume, roses and gardenia, and a trace of tobacco smoke.

As I pull back, we share a look, acknowledging a new settlement. I nod my thanks. I've never seen her without make-up on. It's just one in a whole stream of firsts in the wake of what has happened.

We go inside. Tony can't sit still. Like me he prowls and patrols, pausing to sweep both hands over his head and clutch at his hair. It's a gesture that makes me think of screaming. Of that Munch painting.

Once I've told Tony and Denise everything I can, which is precious little, he fires one question after another at Kay. What are you doing to catch who did this? How did he get in? Did the neighbours see anything? Was it a burglary? Can't they use dogs or something? Have you found Broderick Litton? What about this prowler? He looks older, wrinkled face, pot belly. His hair is thick and wavy still, although there's lots of grey and white among the original bronze colour.

Kay's answers are honest, considered, all disappointing.

He shakes his head, scowling, his mouth tight. He is angry and he is impotent.

Denise doesn't say much, but periodically she goes and touches him, clutches his hand, puts her palm on his chest. Calming him.

I look away.

Florence wakes and sits on Jack's lap. She's subdued, she must be bewildered; my house isn't that big, and it's full of people, including Kay, who she's never met before.

'Kay?' I take her into the kitchen. 'What do we tell Florence?'

'Jack says she didn't see anything?' Kay checks.

'That's right; well,' I amend, 'as far as he knows.' He was out at the gym so it's possible Florence could have seen or heard something. There must have been some noise. Things were broken, weren't they? Why do I think that? My impression of their living room is so sketchy, like a painting where the central subject is clear but everything beyond it is smudged and out of focus.

'She needs to know,' Kay says, 'the simple facts. She might not understand.'

'That makes two of us,' I say bitterly.

Kay regards me steadily. 'She's four, she may not have a concept of death. She needs to understand that Mummy won't be coming back, that her body doesn't work any more, that she won't wake up.'

'I'll get her breakfast first,' I say tersely.

While Florence enjoys the bizarre novelty of having Grandpa Tony and Nana Denise watch her eat her Shreddies, I explain to Jack what Kay has told me.

'I'll do it,' he says. 'Can I take her upstairs?'

'Yes, use my room or the spare room, there's no one staying. If you want me to be there . . .' He shakes my offer away.

It is the longest day. There seems to be no beginning to it and no end in sight. Florence is Jack's shadow, and when it is time to identify the body I have to prise her off him, kicking and screaming. I had hoped to go, wanting to see Lizzie's face, to be certain that the body I'd seen really was my daughter. To make it undeniably real. But Florence needs me here.

Jack's parents, the Tennysons, are on their way from East Anglia, and Tony and Denise have left for now but Tony promised to return later.

After Jack gets back, he tells me that he had to identify Lizzie without looking at her face, which was covered because of the extent of the damage. He had to look at her hands and feet, her wedding ring and the tattoo on her right shoulder: a swallow in flight.

The savagery you must have used. To destroy her face. It astounds me.

Ruth

22

CHAPTER FOUR

17 Brinks Avenue
Manchester
M19 6FX

'Can we go home now?' Florence has a boiled egg with sol-diers. I'm relieved to see her eating. She turns to her father, wiping crumbs from her tiny fingers, a smear of egg yolk on her cheek.

'Not yet,' Jack says.

'When?'

'Another day, I don't know when.'

She thinks about this, a small frown darkening her expres-sion. 'I want Bert.' Bert is Florence's teddy bear. White originally, a gift from Tony and Denise, he is now a muddy grey colour, with bald and ragged ears which Florence liked to chew on as a toddler.

'Can someone fetch it?' I ask Kay. Surely retrieving a child's toy from a different room in the house will not hamper their endeavours, but Kay shakes her head. 'I'll let you know as soon as you can collect anything. Do you have clothes here for Florence?'

'Not really, just the one change for emergencies.' The words die in my mouth. I swallow. 'And a box of toys.' It's kept in one of the kitchen cupboards, but someone got it out earlier and put it in the living room. Florence has ignored it so far.

'Make a list,' Kay says. 'A few basics we can buy. You'll need something too,' she says to Jack. She passes him some paper and a pen.

'I want Bert,' Florence says, her voice rising.

'You'll see Bert soon,' I try to reassure her. 'Perhaps you could look after someone new till then.'

'Who?' she says suspiciously.

'A dolly or a pony? Something from the toyshop. We could go and choose.'

It's touch and go whether she'll play ball or have a tantrum. 'With Daddy,' she says. She doesn't want to be parted from him.

'Of course,' Kay says.

'You'll have to go barefoot,' I say to Florence.

She makes a funny face and I laugh, then feel clumsy and guilty. Lizzie is dead. What sort of mother am I? What sort of human being?

I go with them. I'm not so different from my granddaughter, not keen to let people out of my sight, not comfortable at being left. After all, anything could happen. The world is a chaotic, dangerous, random place now.

We go to John Lewis; it's out of town, with free parking and everything under one roof. We must make a strange sight: Jack and I looking wrecked, slow and distracted, Kay guiding us through the various departments.

We pick a couple of books, familiar ones that Florence has at home, then go to the toy section. Florence stands with her arms folded and surveys the bins of soft toys and the shelves of dolls with disdain. Jack and I make some suggestions: *the little donkey's sweet, how about a polar bear, or the tiger?* She shakes her head each time.

Another child arrives, an older girl, perhaps seven, dressed in a pink pinafore dress and ballet shoes and with fuchsia-pink bows in her hair, dragging a woman, presumably her mother,

24

by the hand. 'This one,' the girl squeals and grabs a baby doll. It's one of those designed to look realistic, with a floppy neck and a protruding navel. There is a range of accessories to buy too, clothes and bottles, nappies and wipes. The woman asks the girl if she's sure, and they move away with their booty.

'Come on, Florence,' Jack says. 'Time to choose.'

Florence goes to one end of the display, then the other, picking up and relinquishing the toys. I can feel something like panic thickening in the air as she darts about.

'You don't have to get one,' I tell her, 'if you don't like them.'

She gives a little shrug. We make it to the escalator, then she turns and runs back. Jack follows her. She picks up one of the lifelike dolls. It's revolting. Staring blue eyes and a pursed rosebud mouth. The wrinkles around its neck and furrows on its forehead make me think of an alien or something old and decrepit.

When we reach the counter, Jack sways. 'I've no card – my wallet . . .' He throws his hands wide.

'I've got mine, no problem,' I tell him.

While Jack goes to get some clothes for himself, I select a few basic outfits for Florence, and spare pyjamas, a coat and some shoes. I barely look at the prices or the designs; all that matters is getting this done, finding the right size.

We go to the supermarket next door – cereal and fish fingers for Florence, a hot chicken, a French stick, wine, bananas, bread and milk.

As I wait to pay, I come close to meltdown. Barely able to stand this: buying food and choosing fruit seems sacrilegious. Irreverent. It's only Florence really that keeps me halfway grounded. As it is, I get my pin number wrong this time. The girl on the checkout looks at us and says very slowly, 'Try it again, love, you get three goes.' She probably imagines we are a care-in-the-community group, practising our basic skills, or refugees of some sort. Which I suppose we are. Except there is no refuge, nowhere to flee. Reality, the reality you brought to our door, is inescapable. Our landscape has altered. We're in the wilderness. You brought it to us.

At home, Florence leaves the doll, discarded, on the floor in the kitchen. After tea, once Jack promises to tuck her in, she lets me bath her. I dress her in her new pyjamas and dry her hair. Abruptly she bursts into tears, wailing, 'I want Mummy.' Her face is creased and red, tears streaming from her eyes and snot bubbling from her nose. I sit her on my lap and rock her and murmur little phrases: 'You're sad, Mummy's dead and she can't come back. Poor Florence. Poor Mummy. Poor Daddy.' I weep too, but silently, not wanting to distress her any more. Gradually her crying fades and stops. She has hiccups.

Downstairs we read one of the books, *We're Going on a Bear Hunt*. Of course we can go to the library and get more on Monday, if Jack and Florence are still here. I've no idea how long it will be until they can go home. I might ask Kay to take her to choose some books. I don't know if I can face people at work. I want to hide away from the world.

Florence insists on sharing a room with Jack, so I tell him to use mine and I'll take the spare room. I fetch some things I'll need, then he puts her to bed and waits until she is asleep and comes downstairs leaving the doors open so we can hear if she cries out.

Kay advises us to only talk to the media with guidance from the police. She says they may ring me, so I put the answerphone on to screen calls.

Lizzie's murder is all over the television news, reports accompanied by a picture of her, cropped from a family photo. Film of their house, sealed off with that tape they use, provides the backdrop for the reporter talking to the camera. They say the same thing each time. 'Greater Manchester Police launched

26

a murder inquiry today after the body of twenty-nine-year-old Lizzie Tennyson was discovered yesterday evening in her home in the Levenshulme area of the city. Lizzie Tennyson was married with one child, and police are asking for anyone with any information to come forward.'

Bea, my oldest friend, is on the doorstep. Her face crumples when she sees me and I pull her inside and she gives me a hug so fierce I think she'll crack my ribs. We go into the lounge. 'I won't stay,' she says, 'unless you—'

'No, thanks.' I shake my head. 'It's crazy.'

'What can I do?' she says. 'Anything, anything at all?'

My mind is blank, woolly. My mobile phone rings. It's been going repeatedly; each time I check the display in case it's Tony. He's the only person I can entertain.

'Ring round people,' I say to Bea. 'Tell them we don't know anything at the moment. When we do, I'll let you know.'

'And I can pass it on.' She's trying so hard not to cry, it tears me up. We're only fit for nods and clenched mouths by way of farewell.

It makes me think of the deaf people Lizzie works with. When tragedy strikes them, do their signs fail, their fingers falter in the same way that words fail the hearing? Lizzie would know. There's a split in my head: part of my brain thinking I must ask her, see what she says, and the other part saying, don't be so bloody stupid, Lizzie's not here any more. And she's never coming back. I think it, I shape the words, but they don't add up. Computer says no. You can't get there from here. My heart cannot keep up with my head and I continually find myself imagining how I will describe all this to Lizzie.

We play the messages on the answerphone at the end of the day. It's agonizing to listen to people's shock and grief and compassion. We make a note of who has rung. There's a message from Rebecca, Lizzie's oldest friend.

27

'I just heard about Lizzie,' she says. 'Oh Ruth, I am so sorry. If there's anything I can do . . .' She starts crying. As a graphic designer, the only job she's found since graduating is in London. She can't afford to rent anywhere in the capital so she's staying with friends, sleeping on their sofa.

I steel myself and ring her back. 'Rebecca, it's Ruth.'

'I'm so sorry,' she says.

'I know. Oh Rebecca.'

'What happened?'

'We don't really know anything yet.' I have learnt that I'm not the only one wanting answers; it's natural to seek understanding, comprehension for something so hard to believe. 'Nothing will happen for a while, with the funeral,' I tell her. 'They, erm . . . they have to wait so an independent post-mortem can be done if there's going to be a trial.'

There has to be a trial, doesn't there? What purgatory would it be to never know who'd hurt Lizzie, to never know the truth?

You were a bogeyman back then. I reinvented you time and again during that long day. The vicious stalker with a fatal obsession, back to carry out your threats. Those sick letters, awful warnings preyed on us all for months. We should have acted, protected her.

Or I pictured you as the prowler, a blurred photofit with dead eyes and jail tattoos, peering in through the windows, sizing up the house, or Lizzie. Watching. Perhaps waiting for Jack to leave. To do what? What were your intentions? Did you plan to take her life, or did something go so terribly wrong that you beat her to keep her quiet?

I wondered if you slept. If you curled up somewhere, safe and warm, muscles relaxing, breath becoming shallow, thoughts fading. Of course I preferred to think of you as frantic, sickened, haunted, like Raskolnikov in *Crime and Punishment*. I had glimpses of you 'coming to your senses', the guilt and horror at what you'd done growing so large as to be unbearable, so you would have to confess. Turn yourself in and beg for forgiveness.

Even then, part of needing to know who you were was because I needed someone to blame. Someone to hate.

Ruth

CHAPTER FIVE

Sunday 13 September 2009

Tony comes back about nine. He comes back and I'm relieved he comes alone. And he and Jack and I drink and talk about Lizzie. An impromptu wake, I suppose.

Our anecdotes are punctuated by expressions of disbelief and sudden urgent questions as we pick over the few stark facts we have. Time and again we are brought up short, confronted by her death. Almost a rhythm to it, waves breaking over us, cold and salty, a merciless tide.

Jack listens intently to the reminiscences that Tony and I share of Lizzie's childhood. The birth was a nightmare, with the baby in distress and me being rushed for an emergency C-section. And it turned our world upside down, not necessarily in a good way at first. The operation left me very weak and it took a long time for me to regain any strength and energy. Which Lizzie snatched from me. She had colic and screamed for hours on end, she kept me marooned in the house, exhausted and weepy and slightly mad. Whenever I managed to get us both up and out, wherever we went, she cried the place down. She failed to thrive, which made me feel like a failure, and I gave up trying to breastfeed, but the formula only seemed to aggravate her colic. We spent money we didn't have trying every possible solution: cranial massage, homeopathy, Reiki healing. Nothing helped.

One night Tony got in late from the salvage yard to find me

weeping in the kitchen and Lizzie screaming in the lounge. The oven had broken, just conked out halfway through baking some potatoes. It was a bitter winter's day, and even with the heating on, the house was chilly. No double glazing or decent insulation back then.

'I'll fix it,' Tony said. He can fix just about anything.

'It'll still take another hour even if you can,' I shouted. 'It's seven already.' Lizzie was still screaming.

'Does she need changing?' Tony said.

'No idea. Why don't you have a look? I'm not doing anything else today. I'm sick of it. Sick of it all.'

He disappeared into the living room. I heard him pick her up, jig her about. The screaming halted for a moment, then resumed.

I lit a cigarette, went outside and smoked it in the perishing wind. I felt cheated: it wasn't meant to be like this.

When I came back in, my eyes watering and my fingers numb, Tony said, 'Get ready, we'll go out to eat.'

'The baby,' I said scornfully.

'My mum's coming round.'

'I don't know if that's—'

'Get ready,' he said, his eyes snapping at me.

'Fine!' I flung back.

I left him mixing formula, Lizzie grizzling in her bouncy chair, and went to change. I felt ugly, lumpen and sullen. My hair greasy and in need of a trim. But I made myself halfway presentable with clothes that didn't reek of baby sick, and when his mother arrived we left her to it.

We went to Rusholme and stuffed ourselves full of curry. The food, the warm buzz of the restaurant, the change of scene worked on me like a tonic. My frustration, my unhappiness ebbed away and I determined to ignore the whisper of anxiety at being away from the baby. We even managed to talk about something other than Lizzie. Tony had been running the architectural salvage business on his own for two years after taking it over from his uncle. He was specializing in interior features: stained glass, wood balustrades, tiles and fire surrounds, cornices and dado rails. In the wholesale rush to convert and modernize, these were being ripped out of old villas and terraces. But some people still valued traditional items, and Tony's business was steadily growing.

From the curry house we went to the pub. We hadn't been out for a drink together since Lizzie was born. After a couple of halves of Guinness, I told him that I definitely wanted to go back to work after my six months' leave, but part time if we could possibly manage it. And I also announced that I didn't want to have any more children. 'I know everyone says that at first,' I told him, 'but I really can't do this again.'

'It's bound to be different,' he said.

'No,' I said, 'because it isn't going to happen. I mean it.' What I was saying was serious and he needed to realize it. 'If you want more kids, you need to be honest with me, and not go along with it thinking I might change my mind. Because I won't.'

'No,' he said, 'I wanted to be a dad, I wanted a child. We've got a child. That's fine.'

I stared at him, into those blue-green eyes, and he met my gaze. He meant what he said.

Florence was so different from Lizzie. Polar opposites. As long as she was fed and clean and warm enough, she was happy. She cried if she needed something but not those raging, painful howls her mother had made, the sort that clawed inside your skull and scraped at your nerves.

'When Lizzie met you,' I say to Jack, 'when you started going out. She was so . . . giddy.'

I remember her bursting to tell us: 'The one who played Cassius, the one with the dark hair.'

Lizzie had been sign-language interpreting at the Royal

Exchange. One of her first big jobs and she was petrified. We were worried at first; Jack was living with someone, but Lizzie insisted that he was an honourable man. He would tell his partner. Of course I fretted: if he could be fickle once . . . But Lizzie knew he was the great love of her life. She never doubted they'd be together.

And she was right. Jack left his girlfriend in London and moved to Manchester.

'And your proposal!' We laugh with delight and another wave of shame runs through me. Lizzie is dead. I ought never to laugh again.

The men catch my mood.

'It's all right,' Tony says, his eyes on me.

'She was embarrassed,' Jack says after a pause.

'But she loved it,' I say. 'The romance of it.' Several months after their first meeting, Jack was playing in *What the Butler Saw* at the Birmingham Rep, and Lizzie was doing the signed performances.

At the end of the show, after the curtain call, Jack remained on stage, and the technician, who'd been primed, played a drum roll, alerting the audience, who were already on their feet ready to leave. Lizzie was sitting at the side of the stage, near the wings.

Jack had practised his message and began to sign to her. At first she did nothing, just went bright red. 'I was too surprised,' she told me. Jack repeated the signs: *Lizzie, I love you. I want to spend the rest of my life with you. Will you marry me?*

Blushing furiously, she stood up and translated to the audience.

A hush of expectation fell over the theatre, broken only by a couple of wolf whistles and someone yelling, 'Say yes.' And answering laughter. Then Lizzie in turn signed to Jack. *Yes, I will. I love you.* And said it aloud. The place erupted with applause and cheers and catcalls.

No one wants to break up our little circle, but eventually at almost two in the morning Tony calls a cab and Jack says good night.

Lizzie was heartbroken when we split up. Is it different for any children? Are there those who find relief in the separation, in the cessation of hostilities? Perhaps.

Lizzie was only fifteen when the mayhem of our troubles clashed with her own teenage trauma. Sometimes it felt like we were three adolescents competing as to who could slam the door hardest, stay silent longest, shout the loudest.

In my memory, that period lasted for years. In reality, it was no more than three or four months. We weren't complete idiots, and even mired in our own pain, we could see how it was hurting Lizzie.

It was the greatest shock of my life.

Before this.

Tony stayed home from work one day. I was doing the late shift at the library and Lizzie had left for school.

'Don't you need to open up?' I said. He had been working all hours, making the most of the lighter nights and a fresh wave of property development in the region.

'I need to talk to you,' he said, a peculiar shifty look on his face.

I had no idea.

We sat at the kitchen table. I swallowed. I couldn't imagine what it was about; my mind alighted on possibilities: financial trouble, a health scare, another discussion about moving house (every few years we'd go through the rigmarole of considering a move, of looking for some wreck and doing it up and selling it on as another way to make some money. But we'd never finally bitten the bullet).

'I've met someone else,' he said.

I stared at him. Clutching at the possibility that I'd misheard,

34

misunderstood. Waiting in case there was something more to come, a punchline, another phrase to set me straight and allow me to breathe again.

When I didn't speak, he cleared his throat. 'It's serious,' he said. His hands, big, brawny hands, clenched together, one nail tugging at a scab.

'Who is it?' I found my voice.

He blinked, his sea-green eyes glittering with something: shame, or embarrassment?

My throat was dry, I stood quickly, went and poured myself a glass of water, took a drink. Turned to him, repeating my question.

'Her name's Denise.'

I didn't know any Denise.

'Where did you meet her, who is she?' My face felt odd, as though I couldn't control my muscles, little tremors flickering through my cheeks, plucking at my lips.

'At physio, she works there.' Tony had hurt his shoulder lifting stuff at work. When it didn't heal, I pestered him until he went to the GP, who referred him on.

I laughed, feeling sick.

'She was looking for a fireplace.'

And got a lover into the bargain.

He exhaled slowly and pulled a face.

'Look, if this is just some fling—' I was ready to forgive, to forget, to retreat. Something was breaking inside me at the prospect that he might leave.

'It's not,' he interrupted. 'I can't stop seeing her, I don't want to stop.'

I turned to look out of the window. I couldn't bear to witness it, what he was saying, the strength of his feeling. 'You bastard,' I said.

'Ruth—'

'Fuck off!' I threw the glass across the room, relishing the sound as it smashed against the wall and water splashed on to the shelves and the floor. 'Get out,' I screeched at him.

He tried to speak, something about sorting things out and Lizzie, but I was incandescent.

That day I called in sick, and I was. Heartsick, wounded. Retreating to my bed, I wept and cursed, all but tore my hair out. What had happened? Obviously he didn't love me as I still did him, but where had it gone? Nineteen years we'd been together. Nineteen.

Lizzie shared my hurt and outrage when Tony and I finally told her what was going on. It would have been easy to form a little cabal, the two of us, to ostracize him, close ranks and sit together picking over his betrayal for our entertainment. Or to force him to choose between Denise and his daughter. But I didn't want to do that. I didn't want to be the stereotype of the cuckolded wife, cold and acerbic and unforgiving. Nor did I want Lizzie to be damaged in the fallout from the split.

Yes, I was hurt, and it took me a long time to feel at peace again in my life. To be comfortable in my solitude. Fourteen years since the parting, and to be honest, there is still a residue there. The scars, perhaps, still niggle and ache.

I've drunk at least a bottle of wine but I am stone-cold sober. I feel bruised everywhere, my muscles aching, my back sore when I stretch or breathe deeply. As if I've been in an accident.

Milky slips up the stairs with me, finds my door shut and yowls and I tell him to hush. He slinks away. When I come into the spare room from the bathroom, he nearly trips me up.

On the pillow, a scrap, bloody strings, half a wing, wet feathers, a beak. A dead chick. I swallow my cry of surprise and fetch tissue paper, take the bird down and put it in the compost bin. Milky at my heels, I retrace my steps.

I spend the night fitfully, frightened to sleep, the cat at my feet. Questions wheeling through my mind: Did she die quickly? Did she suffer? Did she call out, did she speak? What were her last words? *Blunt force trauma.* How many times did he strike her? What with? Was he counting? Did he kick her? Did he rape her? Why kill her, my Lizzie? Why?

When I do let go, my dreams are dark and steeped in blood, my arms full of dead things that I cannot wake.

CHAPTER SIX

17 Brinks Avenue
Manchester
M19 6FX

Early Monday morning, there is a nanosecond of innocent ignorance as I come to and find myself in the spare bed. And then the fist of reality hits like a lump hammer. Shock spikes through me, an electric surge bringing with it an overwhelming feeling that I've done something very, very wrong. Akin to guilt or shame, the emotion sits cold and heavy in the pit of my stomach. Not logical but visceral, and I don't even attempt to analyse it.

No one else is up; it is six o'clock. Outside it is raining, a misty drizzle, and the light is violet grey.

Out of habit, I pour a bowl of muesli and add milk. The first mouthful brings nausea as violent as morning sickness. Mourning sickness? A band of heat around my head, saliva thick in my throat, a spasm rippling up from my stomach.

Restless, feeling confined, I leave a note and go out for a walk. The earliest commuters are about, walking briskly to the train station, or driving past me, sole occupants in their cars. None of the pedestrians speak to me. I keep my eyes averted just in case; we are prone to nods and smiles when we pass each other up here, so this signals that I am not available. I am invisible. A dishevelled grandmother in a sensible waterproof and muddy shoes. Thankfully, I don't meet anyone who recognizes me.

It's as if I'm experiencing everything through a filter, and the rain blurs the world even further. I wander up to the park, ignoring the joggers and the dog-walkers and their animals. In the gloom of the day, a Japanese maple glows luminous red. Reaching the orchard area, I see apples on the trees. Could I eat an apple?

There was a library project we hosted this time last year with the local Sure Start. The children came here and picked apples and then returned to the library for a puppet show about healthy eating and got to polish off their harvest, suitably washed and cored. The trees are labelled. I spot the Cox's orange pippins, my favourite, and twist a small one from the branch, rub the fruit on my jacket and take a bite. It is tart and crisp and stings my taste buds. My eyes water. All those myths, apples that bring evil. Snow White choking, Eve and the snake. I won't be tempting fate. The serpent has already come for me.

The park is full of Lizzie, in her pram, on the climbing frame – though the old one was dull grey metal, four-square, not the wood and rope wigwam that Florence plays on nowadays. Lizzie flat on her back, having a full-blown tantrum, trying to kick me when I went to pick her up, her face red with rage and her hair still a toffee colour before the blonde came in. Blonde like I used to be. My hair now is white, better than grey, but people often assume I'm even older than I am because of it. Lizzie on the field for those family fun days. Later, bigger, huddled on the bowling green benches with her mates, smoking fags.

I manage half the apple before my stomach revolts. I leave the rest for the birds.

Jack and Florence are in the kitchen when I arrive home. She's eating cereal and humming to herself. I can't make out the tune. What on earth is going on in her head? Does she understand what she's been told? Should I talk to her about it as well? I'm not sure I can do it without collapsing in tears. I remember my own high panic and deep unease as a child on the rare occasion my mother cried.

'I've been sent through a summary of the post-mortem,' Kay says when she arrives. 'Would you like Tony to be here? Or I can do it separately?'

'I'll ring him,' I say.

Tony wears the same clothes he had on yesterday. I hesitate, but he moves to me, we hug again, and I'm thankful. We are her parents, after all; no one else can share our perspective. All our arguments and enmity, the bitterness and sorrow, set aside now.

We sit around the kitchen table. More cups of tea. The only thing I can stomach. I have a DVD of *Kung Fu Panda* and I put it on in the living room and leave the door open so that Florence, clinging to Jack's leg, can hear it. It takes a few minutes: she goes through to look and then comes back, twice. The third time she stays there.

'She's checking on you,' I say to Jack, 'in case you disappear as well. Has she said anything?'

'No, nothing.'

I've no idea whether that is a healthy response or not.

Kay has the official papers in her hand. We fall silent and she clears her throat, then reads them to us. 'The post-mortem was carried out yesterday afternoon by Mr Hathaway. He's one of the Home Office pathologists for the region. It began at two fifteen and lasted two and a half hours.'

It's peculiar, but the facts and figures help. Lizzie's murder is impossible to deal with, to frame, but numbers, names, procedures are something to hold on to. Crutches, or footholds in the rock we have to scale. Are we climbing up or climbing down?

40

A peak or a pothole? It is bleak and unmapped, our journey, but these facts are like sparks of light, matches that flame for a second and then gutter out in the fierce wind.

'There was severe blunt force trauma to Lizzie's head, her shoulders, her right arm. A dozen blows at least.'

I start to shake, everywhere, uncontrollably. But I say, 'Go on.'

'The back of her skull was—'

'Do we need this?' Tony bursts out, 'Do we really have to hear—'

'No,' Kay says immediately.

'I do,' I say, 'I want to know. Everything.'

It is true. There's a void, a hunger that can't be sated. The gap left by Lizzie's absence is huge. Unfathomable. I need to fill it with anything I can. Better to fill it with truth than fantasy. No matter how dark the contents of the report are, they will never match what I dredge up in my imagination.

'Tony, if you want to wait?' Kay says.

'It's fine . . . just . . .' Tony clamps his hands over his mouth and squeezes his eyes shut tight.

Jack is silent, ashen, trembling as I am.

'The back of Lizzie's skull was crushed with multiple fractures, the right orbital socket around the eye was fractured, as well as the nose and the right ulna – in the arm. Cause of death was due to blunt force trauma. It is likely that she died as a result of one of the early blows.' I wonder how they can possibly know that.

'The weapon was long and narrow, cylindrical, almost certainly the poker that was recovered from the scene,' Kay says.

'Oh God,' I breathe.

'Poker?' Tony says. The fire irons. Genuine antiques. Tony gave them to Lizzie and Jack when they put the wood-burner in. You can get modern ones almost identical, black cast iron. Long-handled shovel, tongs, brush and poker.

Jack presses his fist to his head, closing his eyes for a moment. 'There could be fingerprints?' he says, looking at Kay.

'Were there any on the poker?' I ask.

'I don't know,' Kay says. 'It will take some time for us to have forensic results back, but fingerprints are one of the first things to be recovered and examined. The CSIs will also look for footwear impressions, palm prints, anything they can find. And DNA traces on Lizzie's body. Her body has been swabbed and her hair brushed, scrapings taken from under her nails. These are all areas where the attacker may have left traces that can help us to identify him.'

'Was she raped?' My voice is uneven.

Jack stiffens, and Tony hunches over in his seat.

'There is no sign of that.' Kay waits to see if we have any other questions before continuing. 'There's something else that the post-mortem revealed. Lizzie was pregnant.'

'No!' Jack says.

Tony and I look at each other, both bewildered.

'Seven weeks' gestation. Twins. You didn't know?' she says to Jack.

He shakes his head, tears welling in his eyes.

The reverberations from that bombshell echo in the silence that follows. All the futures that might have been. Brothers or sisters or both for Florence; Lizzie pushing a double buggy. The hope and promise of new babies.

Jack gets up abruptly and goes upstairs. We can hear him being sick, a raw, retching sound.

'What about Broderick Litton?' Tony says.

'We've not been able to trace him yet.'

'Why not?' I say. 'All the surveillance we have, cameras everywhere, bureaucracy, the internet.'

'If people want to stay under the radar, it's possible,' Kay says.

I think about it: no wages or NI, no GP or car registration, no bank account. You'd have to live on the streets.

'We are looking,' she says.

I wonder where you are. Where you can hide. If you have gone on the run, to London, or Spain, or across the globe. Or perhaps you are still here, in Manchester, watching the news updates, relieved as Lizzie's murder drops off the headlines and the front pages. Do you find an excuse to change channels when it's on or are you audacious enough to make observations about it? I hope you are paralysed with fear. Unable to eat or sleep or think. Counting the minutes till there's a knock on the door and they come for you.

Ruth

CHAPTER SEVEN

Monday 14 September 2009

Jack's parents arrive, Marian and Alan; Jack saw them briefly at their hotel last night. After a tactful few minutes sharing commiserations and expressions of shock and sad disbelief, I leave them to it, ask them to excuse me if I go and lie down. There are too many people in the house as it is, and I think they need some space to talk with their son. I'm also worried that if I don't stop for a little while, I'll physically collapse. I've never been a fan of melodrama, and me keeling over would only be an added strain for everyone.

My heart is painful in my chest, a dull ache as if it's swollen, and pounding too fast. I take my slippers off and lie on my back on the bed and try to slow my breathing, to release the knots in my stomach, the slab of tension across my back. It doesn't work: as soon as I lose concentration, which I do easily, I find myself holding my breath. Dredging up some moves from yoga from years ago, I try those, but it's hopeless. My body rebels, taut, spastic.

Closing my eyes, I focus on the sounds: birds in the garden, a bus wheezing by, the sound of someone clinking pots from downstairs, the ticking of the central heating radiator, sibilant fragments from Florence's DVD. There is some tinnitus in my ears, a revolving hum that may be a machine somewhere but is probably just a noise in my head.

Should I see the GP about the burning pain in my chest? I'm

on medication already for high cholesterol. Someone mentioned the GP, Tony or Kay, I can't remember now. For tranquillizers or sleeping pills. *The poker. A dozen blows. Twins.* Like the whirring in my ears, the images, the details tumble around.

This was Lizzie's room.

The place where she had her cot, though her incessant crying meant that for much of the first year she slept in with me while Tony managed on a mattress on the floor in here. When she was walking and talking, the crying eased and we moved her into this room. She outgrew the cot, had a child's bed. Then came bunk beds and sleepovers, posters on the walls and a desk for homework. So fast. It all went so fast.

The room has changed now: once Lizzie moved out for uni, I did it up. Started taking temporary lodgers, actors up for work at the Lowry or the Royal Exchange, Contact or the Palace. There's a small TV and DVD in here for the lodgers. If we get on well, we watch some programmes together on the big set downstairs. Having the company is nice, and when I have the place to myself again, I enjoy the freedom. It helps pay the bills, and I've met some lovely people over the years, only one or two idiots. I also get to see an awful lot of theatre.

'DI Ferguson wants to meet you,' Kay tells us. 'She is leading the investigation. Will this afternoon be all right? What about Tony?'

'I'll check with him,' I say.

'Have you had anything to eat?' she asks.

'I can't face it.'

'Some soup,' she suggests. 'Your friend Bea called while you were resting. She brought some leek and potato. And a French stick.'

'I need to ring her.'

'She said she'll come round tonight unless you text her,' Kay says.

'Where are the others?'

'They've taken Florence to the library.'

'The library?'

'That all right?' Kay says. 'They asked her where she'd like to go and that's what she said.'

It makes sense. Somewhere familiar, safe, welcoming. The staff know Florence through me, and Jack takes her to the story sessions and the events we have there. I'm about to reply, to tell Kay something about the library and my lifelong job there, when the pain in my chest ratchets up several notches and my head swims. I put out my hand but there's nothing there to hold on to, and I feel myself swooning, falling back, my bones gone to water.

The GP, someone from my practice I'd never met, listens to my heart and takes my blood pressure. He knows the situation and advises me to try and eat, little and often, and increase my fluid intake. He thinks I'm dehydrated as well as suffering from shock and stress. 'Your heart sounds fine, no arrhythmia; your blood pressure is high, but that's to be expected. I'm not unduly worried.' Doctor speak. *Unduly.* Who else says *unduly* these days?

He writes a prescription for a mild tranquilliser in case I need it.

'What about side effects?' I say. 'Is it addictive?'

'Not with a short course at this dosage,' he says. 'There are a range of potential side effects. The leaflet lists them all, but the most common ones are feelings of detachment . . .'

Isn't that the point?

'. . . drowsiness, and a dry mouth.'

Do I want to feel detached? If I muffle the emotions, won't they just grow in intensity, waiting to ambush me when I stop taking the medicine? 'I'm not sure I want it,' I tell him.

'Entirely up to you; the script is valid for six months, anyway. And if there's anything else you need, do ring the surgery.'

Marian and Alan bring Florence back; she's clutching a pile of picture books that threaten to overbalance her. They plan to do some shopping for us. Marian is brisk and practical and talks too much, a running commentary. She's probably afraid that she'll fall to pieces if she stops. Alan's reserved, speaks only to agree with her comments or echo her thoughts. We've only met them a handful of times, at the wedding, once before that and then at Florence's first birthday party. I watch Marian heating the soup and talking about allotments and gardens. And home-cooked vegetables. She manages to talk about soup for a good five minutes.

Living in East Anglia, they see much less of Jack and Lizzie and Florence than Tony or I do. What will happen now? Would Jack think of leaving, go and live there, take Florence? The thought sends panic swirling through me, and I grip the table. When they're ready to leave for the shops, I ask Marian if she will fill the prescription for me.

I can't cope with all the people calling at my house to comfort us. It seems heartless to turn them away, but Kay suggests she act as gatekeeper and will explain that we are grateful for their good wishes but too distressed to meet anyone.

Cards arrive, from neighbours and colleagues and friends. It takes me ten minutes and several tours of the house to find my reading glasses. I keep losing things. As if now that I have lost Lizzie, I can't keep hold of anything else.

I open a batch of cards at the table.

'Is it your birthday?' Florence says, her head cocked to one side.

'No. These cards are for us because of Mummy dying. People know we're sad. They're thinking about us.' Her face closes down and she slips from the chair. I go after her into the lounge.

'Where's Daddy?' she says.

'Gone for a shower. It's all right to be sad,' I say. 'Everyone's sad.'

'I'm not,' she says. 'This book.' She pulls out a battered copy of *Each Peach Pear Plum*, still doing the rounds. I remember reading it to Lizzie.

'Okay.' I sit on the sofa and she clambers on to my lap.

We say the words together, and she tilts her head from side to side as she chants, pointing with her finger at the characters hidden in the pages. Mother Hubbard, Cinderella, Robin Hood.

And for a few minutes Florence and I escape, float down the river with Baby Bunting, tumble down the hill with Jack and Jill and climb through the branches of the great tree.

CHAPTER EIGHT

17 Brinks Avenue
Manchester
M19 6FX

DI Ferguson takes my hand in both of hers when we meet, her grasp firm. She looks me in the eyes and says, 'I'm so sorry. We are doing everything possible to establish what happened to Lizzie and bring whoever is responsible to justice.' She glances around. 'Is Mr Tennyson here?' she says to Kay.

'I'll get him. Tony, Mr Sutton, will be here any time.'

We go in the dining room. I call it that but no one ever eats in here. I use it for overspill, for hobbies and storage. The inspector takes her jacket off and drapes it over the back of an armchair. She's small next to Kay, close to my height though slimmer than me. A black woman, her clothes stylish, her hair pulled up away from her face in a topknot. Specs, red and white and brown patterned frames, on a chain round her neck. A touch of pinky-red lipstick.

She has a pent-up energy to her as though she's idling and ready to take off at speed. It's there in the intensity of her gaze, eyes bright, and the pace of her speech. In repose there is a hint of a smile about her mouth, as though life is everything she hoped it would be. She stands and greets Jack and Tony.

When everyone is settled, DI Ferguson says, 'I'm the senior

investigating officer, and that means I'm in charge of the inquiry into Lizzie's murder. Kay will remain your liaison officer and she'll pass on to you any significant information, but I want you to know that if you ever need to speak to me directly, if you've any concerns or questions that Kay can't answer, please get in touch. I'll leave my card before I go. What happened to Lizzie,' she says, 'is simply unforgivable.'

I try not to weep, because I need to hear what she has to say.

'No one should lose a wife, a daughter, a mother, a friend in that way. From your position you may feel as though there is little news, as if things are not moving quickly enough but I want to reassure you that we are making steady progress. The results of the post-mortem, which Kay related to you, have given us the cause of death but also flagged up a number of forensic items of interest which we are now examining. The same goes for the evidence recovered from the scene at the house. But it's not like on television. Some of the forensic tests we need to do will take several days to be completed, sometimes weeks. They can't be rushed. They have to be done to an exacting standard, robust enough for prosecution.'

'Lizzie's phone,' I say, thinking of that text she sent me. 'Did she try and call for help?'

'No. Her phone was recovered from the house. There was no activity from her after the text she sent to you,' says DI Ferguson.

No chance to use her phone, perhaps she was oblivious to the danger. Perhaps she never knew what was coming. I think of Florence asleep as the carnage unfolded downstairs. Kay has asked her if she saw or heard anything the night Mummy was hurt but Florence simply shook her head.

'Our door-to-door inquiries are continuing as well, and calls from the general public are being fed into the investigation and followed up. Officers are examining footage from

CCTV cameras in the vicinity to see if the perpetrator can be identified.'

'Broderick Litton?' I say.

'We've not found him yet,' says DI Ferguson.

'He's out there,' Tony says hotly, 'and . . .' He crumples.

'I can assure you we are making every effort to find him, and as soon as we do, you will know about it.' She turns to Jack. 'We have traced and interviewed the man who broke into your neighbour's property on the Tuesday night. He admits to also having entered your garden on Wednesday.'

I hold my breath.

'But we have eliminated him from our inquiries.'

'How come?' Jack says.

'He has a watertight alibi for the Saturday evening.'

'Are you sure?' Jack says.

'Yes,' says DI Ferguson.

Questions toll in my head again: *who, why, how?*

'Is there anything we can do?' Tony says.

DI Ferguson gives a nod. 'There are two ways you might help, but I want to stress that there is no obligation on any of you to do so. Different families react very differently, and what is right for someone else may not be right for you.'

'What are they?' Jack says.

'We would like your help with a fresh appeal to the general public. A quote from you about Lizzie, saying what sort of person she was, would be very helpful. We want to keep the public involved in assisting us, we want to make her as real as possible to people who have never met her. There is already a high degree of interest because of the circumstances of Lizzie's murder, because she was an ordinary young woman, a mother, expecting to be safe in her own home.'

Like we all do.

'Also, well-wishers have been leaving flowers outside the house. If this is something you would like to do, we can arrange

51

that, and if you are willing, we'd like to film your visit and that would form part of a new press release. Again, that's entirely up to you.'

'You want to keep it in the news?' Tony says.

'That's right. I certainly do,' DI Ferguson says keenly.

'Yes, we'll help,' I say, looking to Jack, who nods his agreement.

'Yes,' says Tony.

'Thank you. Kay will go over the details. Now, is there anything you want to ask me? If I can answer you, I will.'

Marian and Alan arrange takeaways for our meal that evening. My table only seats four, but we crowd round it, joined by Tony and Denise. Jack tells his parents what we'll be doing for the appeal, then people make gentle conversation, mainly on safe topics. We're all too numb to exchange any more reactions about Lizzie's death. The medication has kicked in, making me feel dopey.

Marian and Alan go back to their hotel, Kay goes home, Tony and Denise leave and Bea arrives. We hug for a long time. Death does this: suddenly human touch, physical expressions of comfort and warmth, is instinctive. Freely given and received.

We settle in the kitchen and Bea makes coffee. 'God, Ruth, I don't know what to say. It still doesn't seem real.'

'Not even to me, and I saw her. Perhaps if I'd been able to go and identify her . . .' *A dozen blows at least.* Her face.

'Will they let you see her another time?'

I shrug.

'Ask them,' she says.

'She was pregnant, Bea.'

Her lip quivers.

I try and keep my voice steady. 'Twins, not far on, seven weeks.'

'Oh Ruth, it's horrendous. Whoever it is, I hope he's shot resisting arrest or something.' She slams the cafetière down on the side and I fear the glass will crack.

'No. Don't say that.'

'Why?' She's almost cross with me.

'Because then we won't know anything.'

She baulks, considering this, raises her eyebrows. 'Perhaps it's best—'

'No,' I interrupt, 'it isn't.'

I try and explain to her.

In the night I wake and hear crying, sobbing, Jack in the other bedroom. No sound from Florence. Poor, poor man.

I wonder whether she knew her fate. Whether she sensed it as the door swung open. She was good at reading body language; intrinsic to her work after all. But she was shy, too, reserved, so that might have been a check on her instinctive response.

At what point did she know? Or did she die ignorant, oblivious? You must have had time to grab the poker, or did you attack her before you picked that up? Trip her over, knock her down, punch her?

One of the hardest things is imagining the terror she must have felt if she did realize you were going to hurt her. If she understood with the innate sense of an animal that she was in jeopardy, in the deepest danger. The preservation of life is the strongest instinct; it's why starving people will eat their young, why someone trapped will sever their own limb.

Had she the prescience to know her life was ending? It pierces my soul to think of Lizzie riddled with that level of fear.

When you finally answer my questions, I hope that you will tell me that she had no notion of what would befall her, that you tricked her and she turned away, and she never saw you raise the cast-iron stick. That the first blow felled her like a lamb, crushed her brain like a grape, stopped her heart, the swelling of her lungs, the blood in her veins. I hope that you will tell me that.

But I need you to tell me the truth.

However bleak.

Ruth

CHAPTER NINE

Thursday 17 September 2009

Kay orders the flowers. A bouquet from Jack, one from Tony and me. She brings back some stationery too, cream vellum, thick, for us to write notes.

Florence is drawing a rainbow with felt tips, upper teeth snagging her lower lip in concentration. She presses hard on the paper, which begins to tear. When I try to slide another piece of paper underneath, she shoves it away. I feel a moment's fierce irritation. Hold it in. After all, the kitchen table is already marked with scratches, burns and scuffs, biro marks. A bit of felt tip won't hurt.

I pick up a pen and stare at the paper. What can I possibly say? 'I can't do this,' I mumble, tears stinging the back of my eyes. I pull my glasses off.

'Ruth . . .' Tony says.

'No.' I go outside. Words have been my life, words, books, stories, reading. Okay, maybe not the whole of my life, but a great part of it, and now they fail me. They are inadequate, pale, flimsy, weak.

Tony comes out after a few minutes. 'We can just keep it simple,' he says. 'Say we love her, always.' His voice wavers and he pinches his nose.

'It's not enough.'

'A poem then, a quotation.'

I smile, a rush of affection. I used to send him poems when

we first started going out. Sonnets and verses I thought he'd like. Shakespeare, Donne, Plath, Dickinson.

'I'll have a look.'

He had come to the library looking for reference books about architecture, wanting to become more knowledgeable for his salvage work. I had just started there, librarian assistant on a job creation scheme. A way to get off the dole for six months. After a degree in English and history and a year's teacher training, I decided that teaching was not for me. At least not classroom teaching. But I loved the library work, helping people with all sorts of quests for knowledge.

When Tony asked for advice, whether there were any more books he could get hold of, I suggested he try Central Library with its extensive reference section. I showed him how to find books in the catalogue and, if they weren't in our Ladybarn branch, how to request an inter-library loan.

He kept coming back. Shelley, one of the other staff, nudged me one day: 'Romeo's in again.' I wondered who she meant. Then she nodded to him. 'Put him out of his misery, Ruth, ask him out.'

'You don't think . . .' I blushed.

'I do. Don't you like him?'

It took me a moment to answer. 'Yes.'

'Well then. Invite him to the Valentine's Verse Night.' We were having an event with local poets and musicians.

My face was still aflame as Tony came up to the counter.

'This one's overdue,' he said. 'My uncle borrowed it.'

'First time, I'll let you off.'

He smiled. When he smiled, his green eyes shone.

Tony isn't traditionally handsome; he certainly hasn't got the leading-man looks that Jack has. He's well built, broad-shoul-dered, with huge hands and feet. A bit like a prop forward. His nose is sharp, his cheeks round. He had curly blond hair back then but I found him attractive. And he had charisma.

There was also the appeal of his attention; he was really interested in me, in my opinions. We had long discussions, arguing about politics and feminism and social issues; he teased me about my middle-class background and I teased him back about his Manchester scally posturing. He was easily as bright as I was, which was what really mattered.

I fell in love with him.

I didn't ever stop, though I've learnt to hide it. I still don't know, don't really know, what Denise gives him that I didn't. Why he prefers her. Objective as I can be, I don't get it. I never have.

We are all tense; the atmosphere in the house before we leave to lay the flowers is brittle.

The rain has stopped, but it's cold and damp and the feel of winter is in the air. Jack looks wiped out, purple shadows under his eyes. On the way in the car he starts shivering, and I reach out and touch him. The look he gives me is so sad, so wretched, I almost ask if we can call the whole thing off.

Jack has white flowers, roses, gypsophila, lilies and carnations. The carnations smell strong, sweet and spicy in the car. Melissa and Mags have been to the allotment and gathered some wild flowers – cornflower, little daisies, cow parsley and sweet peas –included in the florist's arrangement of yellow roses and blue iris that I carry.

Florence is with us; she has brought a new picture, a drawing of Milky, though if you weren't primed you'd be hard put to tell it was an animal at all, let alone a cat.

We have our instructions. Jack and Florence will go first, walk down the pavement and leave the bouquet and picture. Then Tony and I will join them; we will go together in a show of solidarity to reinforce that Lizzie was from a loving home. It smacks of hypocrisy to me. This focus on how wholesome Lizzie was. The deserving and the undeserving dead.

'There's a story,' Jack said when Kay talked us through the

sequence and Tony asked about Denise being involved too. 'You keep the story simple.' Denise wants to pay her respects, so Tony has agreed to visit with her after we have all been. She is a complicating factor.

I'm taken aback to see so many reporters and film crews crowded at the end of the cul-de-sac.

Jack places his flowers down beside all the other bunches there. Florence puts her picture next to it. Then we are told it's our turn. It is hard to concentrate; my mind keeps jumping back to that night, to Jack and Florence at this spot, the front door ajar. To my Lizzie, so still on the floor.

Getting my glasses out, I make an effort to read the cards that have been left, but time and again my mind slides away. Florence raises her arms and Jack picks her up. She lays her head on his shoulder.

Across the road the waiting journalists do their stuff, a buzz of activity and attention, a continual rippling, click and chime of cameras. Cigarette smoke on the air.

'Can we get Bert now?' Florence says.

'No,' Jack says, 'not yet.'

The house is still off limits.

There is a giddy sensation inside me. I feel close to the edge, as if I might suddenly do something grossly inappropriate, fart or vomit or burst out laughing. I clench my teeth until my head aches.

We walk back to the car, a sad little procession, then Florence kicks off, wrenching round in Jack's arms, pointing back to the house and crying.

'What is it?' he asks her. 'What do you want?'

She is screaming and it's hard to make out the words.

Jack glances at me to see if I have any idea what's going on. I shake my head.

'We have to go to Nana's,' Jack tells her. 'We can't go home yet.'

'I know!' she bawls.

'Show me,' Jack says, and lowers her to the ground. Florence runs back and we follow. She snatches up her picture. The crying softens to small sobs.

'You want to bring it?' I say.

She nods her head.

'That's fine. You keep it.' Then I do laugh, half laugh, half cry. My throat painful.

We leave again.

We look peculiar on the television, Tony and I. If I didn't know us, had to guess what we did, who we were, I'd say he was a stevedore. Hah! Not much call for stevedores in Manchester in the twenty-first century. A forklift truck driver then, or a brickie. His weathered complexion, solid build, those peasant's hands. And me? I don't know. With white hair to my shoulders, the specs and the middle-aged spread, I look older than I feel, older than I really am.

One or two of the reports give more details about Lizzie and Jack. Jack has done some television, guest parts on *Casualty* and *The Bill*, as well as his theatre roles. But he's not a household name. There would be even more attention if he was.

The camera pans over our bouquets propped up against the garden wall, the cards and notes in plastic sleeves, the messages of love, our blessings. A voiceover relates our description of Lizzie: *Lizzie was a much-loved daughter, wife and mother, a warm and loving person who lived life to the full. Her passion for theatre and the arts . . .* The film focuses on Florence's drawing, a row of kisses at the bottom, on Jack's note, *my love forever*; it moves to our signatures, *Mum* and *Dad*, beneath the verse from Christina Rossetti's poem, 'Echo', just out of sight.

Come to me in the silence of the night;
Come in the speaking silence of a dream;
Come with soft rounded cheeks and eyes as bright

As sunlight on a stream;
Come back in tears,
O memory, hope, love of finished years.

CHAPTER TEN

Friday 18 September 2009

DI Ferguson was right, it does seem as though nothing is happening. Stasis. We go through the motions of eating and drinking; we wash, though I'm tempted not to bother. As though wearing my dirt on my skin and letting my hair grow greasy and tangled can serve as symbols of my distress and sorrow. It makes sense. I understand now those newscasts from other countries: the rending of clothes, the tearing of hair, the howls of grief. *See how I hurt, I will hurt myself to show you.*

But we are British. And there is Florence to think of. It would all be so different without her. I could indulge myself, not beholden to anyone. Rave and rage and lose control.

Jack signals to me and we move into the hall.

'What do we do about school?' he says quietly.

'I don't know. The routine . . .' I begin thinking perhaps it would help Florence then I falter. I have no idea what is best. She is settling in well there, in reception, moving up from the school's nursery class, and usually looks forward to going, but I can't quite imagine a bereaved child returning to school so soon.

'We can ask Kay,' I say.

Kay's advice is to see what Florence wants to do. If she wants to go in, Kay will speak to the school and explain the situation.

'I'll take her,' Jack says, 'if she wants to go. I usually take her.'

When Jack asks Florence about school, she says no, alarm in her voice.

'Okay,' Jack agrees, 'you'll go another day, maybe.'

'No,' she says again.

He glances at me, I shrug. What can we do?

Tony returns to work. Does that sound heartless? He tells me he is going mad with nothing to do, brooding at home. That he'll be better occupied, his business won't run itself, though they could get by on Denise's income for a few weeks if they had to. There is no way I can face the thought of work, but I force myself to go out of the house once a day. I cannot hide for ever.

Returning the calls of people who have left messages is really difficult, and I give up trying.

'You've not been able to have a funeral yet,' Kay says. 'Usually when someone dies you can focus on that, you're run ragged making arrangements, everything's leading to saying a very public goodbye. Without that it is hard to move on with grieving.'

She is right, we are rudderless. 'People will understand and you can get in touch when you're ready. Don't sweat it.'

Kay has a few Americanisms that make me smile. She spent some time working over there on an exchange programme. In Chicago. She loved it.

'You wouldn't go back?'

'No chance now, they're not hiring.'

The tablets help in one regard: they make it easier for me to avoid dwelling on the scene at Lizzie's house. It is there at the edge of my mind, a shadow hovering, but like a word that can't be summoned, or a name forgotten, it stays just out of reach. Sometimes I wake suddenly, full of unease, sweating, and I wonder if I've been dreaming about Lizzie, visiting the scene in my slumber. Jack hasn't taken any medication though I suggest he might. I hear him crying most nights, or pacing about.

We do everything we are asked. Jack talks to the police again.

Every day I ask Kay if they've had any witnesses come forward, if anyone saw anything, a stranger in the area. If they've found Broderick Litton.

'Nothing yet, but it is very early on,' she keeps saying.

My neighbours bring more food. We've already had to throw some out and I've no idea which dishes are whose.

Jack puts a lasagne in the oven.

'Did the police say anything?' I ask him.

He shakes his head, and then stills. 'Only that they think she let him in.'

My heart quickens. Another morsel of fact. They are like shots of a drug. Dizzying, addictive. 'Why do they think that?' I sit down.

'Because there wasn't any damage to the door, no sign of him breaking in anywhere else.'

I absorb this. 'She would never have let that man in. Litton. Not in a million years. Or anyone else, come to that.'

'I know,' Jack says. 'I told them.'

'He might have forced his way in as soon as she opened the door,' I say.

We look at each other, Jack tightens his mouth and the dimple in his chin deepens.

Kay encourages me to talk about Lizzie. About her before all this. I'm not sure at first; it's painful until I get lost in the stories. Gradually I see that it's healthy to shift the focus away from Lizzie's death to the rest of her life, all those twenty-nine years. To take her off the pedestal too: not some alabaster martyr, flawless and sublime, but a person who made mistakes and could be infuriating at times.

I tell Kay about the colic and the trials of teenage-hood, which I'm sure was normal enough but was a nightmare at the time. About how stubborn Lizzie could be even if she was in the wrong, and the raging rows she'd have particularly with Tony. And I explain how we came through all that. That the good times far outweighed the hard ones and I took such delight in her, her talents and her character and her generous spirit.

At sixteen she had an abortion after getting pregnant by some boy she had only dated for a month. Of course we'd have supported her whatever she chose to do, but I was relieved when she opted for a termination. She was so young, still a child herself in many ways. I was ready to go with her to the clinic, but she wanted to take her friend Rebecca instead. She was sad after the procedure, naturally – she sat beside me on the sofa and cried, and I rocked her in my arms – but she never regretted the choice.

CHAPTER ELEVEN

17 Brinks Avenue
Manchester
M19 6FX

Perhaps you are ill, mentally ill, I think, as I sit and open more cards and letters. Wouldn't you have to be to stalk my daughter like you did? To come back and kill her? Though I know about the stereotypes. Most people with a mental illness are more likely to be the victims of violence than the instigators. Or to hurt themselves. The *Daily Mail* notion of the mad axeman is extremely rare. And these days it's more likely to be a ceremonial sword.

At work, our doors are open to everyone, and some of the library users have health problems, mental or physical or both. In past times they'd have been locked up in asylums. I can't imagine any of them attacking someone. Not Ruby, who is highly educated and speaks half a dozen languages and trembles like a butterfly, anxiety singing in every cell of her body. Or Giles, who lived with bipolar. 'I'm manic-depressive,' he announced when I first met him. 'If I get on your nerves, just tell me to sod off. I do witter on sometimes.' Giles wrote poetry, sheaves of it. He had romantic stories published in women's magazines, and when he was well enough, he attended the creative writing group the WEA ran at the library. One summer's night he lay down on the train tracks outside Levenshulme station and ended his life. He was a lovely man.

65

But perhaps you are the exception, the one in a million who won't take their meds and who runs amok and kills a stranger. The attack on Lizzie was vicious, sustained. Were there voices in your head commanding you to strike? Again and again. Why Lizzie? Why stalk her? Why come and kill her? Are women the enemy? Do you hate all women, or just young, pretty ones?

The sun shines as I walk up to the park. I avoid the shops, haven't been in to buy anything. No hurry.

I am at the duck pond when someone calls my name.

Squinting into the sun, I see him. Hoodie up, pants halfway down his bum showing his boxers, trainers in some bright electric blue. Doddsy, one of the lads from the basic skills group who used to meet at the library. In his early twenties now. School had failed him but he had enough nous to try a different route when given the opportunity.

'Hello, Doddsy.'

'Sorry about your daughter. It's really . . . just . . .' he says, flushing.

My chest tightens. 'Thanks. How are you?'

'Good. Got this mentor now and I'm doing a sound production course. Well good.'

'That's great,' I say.

'Yeah. If I can help, you know, if there's anything . . .'

'Thanks.'

'Better go.' He shrugs, and shuffles his feet. 'See ya.'

I smile and nod, touched by his kindness.

Something shifts as I realize that not only have you taken Lizzie's life and shattered ours, not only have you turned Lizzie from an ordinary person into a victim, but you have twisted my identity as well. Warped it. For ever more, for most people I will be Ruth, the woman whose daughter was killed. The mother of a murder victim. That's what people will see first and above everything else; that's how people will talk about me, will name me.

What is even more sickening is that it's a role I've embraced in these last four years. Because of my hatred, my thirst for revenge, my greed to see you suffer. My obsession. I have allowed myself to disappear into the role of bereaved parent.

And that is partly why I'm writing to you. I want to be more than that. Break that typecasting.

They say no man is an island, they say we're a construct of all the roles we play, but I am so very, very tired of this one.

You have brought such bitterness to my door. Filled my veins with such violent animosity and my heart with such hate that I can barely recognize myself any more. I want to find the old Ruth, the Ruth who cursed her screaming baby and rowed with her teenage daughter, the bibliophile who fell in love and copied out poems and learnt to grow vegetables and had a penchant for soul music and chocolate and liked cats.

You've done your level best to kill her too, but she's not dead yet, not completely.

Ruth

CHAPTER TWELVE

17 Brinks Avenue
Manchester
M19 6FX

Six days. What's that in hours? I work it out. One hundred and forty-four. It feels longer. Although time is a pretty nebulous concept, the hours and days bleed together. How many seconds? How many heartbeats?

Had you any idea the police were closing in on you? Or as the days rolled by did you breathe easily, and dare to hope you'd got away with it?

Florence has not touched the doll since she brought it home. She keeps trying to cuddle Milky, hauling the poor animal up with her arms under his stomach. He's placid, won't scratch or bite her, but he thrashes about and runs off.

Florence and I are alone. Florence is at the table eating some beans on toast. Kay has a meeting with the investigation team, Jack's having a rest. We are still stumbling through our lives. I'm sorting through some clean clothes left neglected in the basket. Even this simple task seems to require a Herculean effort.

One of my socks, old grey wool, has a hole in the toe. No point in keeping it. I stick my hand in, wiggle my finger through the hole, put on a funny fluting voice. 'Hello.' I make the sock bow.

'What is it?' says Florence.

'I don't know. Maybe . . .' I gather the fabric and narrow it into a windsock shape, 'maybe it's a Clanger.'

'What's a Clanger?'

'They were on the telly a long time ago. Lived on a planet with a soup dragon. They made a noise like this.' I combine a hum and a whistle.

'I want a Clanger,' she says. 'No – I want a sock cat. No – a kitten.'

'A kitten, eh? What would it need?'

'Some ears.' She scoops up the last of her beans.

'And whiskers?'

'Yes, and paws.'

My sewing skills are basic. 'Paws might be tricky. Let's see . . .'

The sewing box yields enough black felt scraps to furnish two triangular ears and two round eyes, Florence chooses a brown leather button for a nose.

'Look at Milky's eyes,' I say. Milky is sitting on the chair by the radiator. Florence kneels up in front of him and stares. Milky yawns, affecting disdain, but then his ears flatten and I can see he's preparing for a rapid exit if she makes a lunge. 'Yellow bits,' she says.

'What shape?'

She sketches something unreadable with her hands.

'Great.'

I have some yellow cotton and use that to stitch a vertical line on the eyes. Plaited brown wool furnishes a tail. There's nothing stiff enough for the whiskers, so we make do with more lengths of the wool, which hang down like a droopy moustache, but Florence seems happy.

'She needs insides,' Florence says. 'She's all flat.'

'If we leave it empty, it can be a puppet,' I say.

'I don't want a puppet,' she scowls. 'Not a puppet!' Suddenly cross.

'Okay.'

A couple of J Cloths, torn into strips, serve as stuffing. I sew the top of the sock shut, biting the thread to cut it. 'There we go.'

Florence bounces the kitten along the table.

'What will you call it?'

'Kitten.'

'Okay, highly original.'

'No, Kit Kat,' she says.

'Right.'

'No . . .' She purses her mouth and furrows her brow as she thinks. 'Matilda.'

Where's this come from? Has she had the book? Seen the film? The little girl who is neglected and bullied at home and school but who finds secret powers and blossoms in the love and care of her teacher.

'Yes,' she says firmly, 'Matilda.'

The door opens and I look up, expecting Lizzie, come to collect Florence. Tired from her journey but glad to be working, with stories from her day.

I have forgotten, which means I have to remember anew. A lance in my heart. Swallowing the cry in my mouth, I fight to smile at Jack.

Florence is in the living room with Kay, CBBC on the television. There is talk of the BBC moving to Manchester. Jack hopes it will happen; it might provide more work for him.

'We should think about getting her back to school,' I say.

'I don't think she'll wear it,' Jack says.

'She'll have to sooner or later, unless you plan to home-school her.'

He gives me a sceptical look.

'A phased return,' I say. 'We can work something out with the staff. Who is it, Mrs Bradshaw?'

'Yes.'

'Even if we have to go and sit in with her for a month. You've no work lined up?' I ask him.

'No,' he says, 'I've not had an audition since I went up for *The History Boys*. I should speak to Veronica, tell her the situation.'

Veronica is his agent. 'She'll have heard,' I say. 'There's time.'

'I should get a phone,' he says. Like Bert the teddy bear, Jack's phone was in the house and is off limits for now.

I get a glimpse of all the practicalities Jack will have to face, rearranging work and childcare around Florence, sorting out the house: he will want to move, surely, find somewhere new, neutral, not tainted with Lizzie's murder. And then all their financial affairs and all the connections of Lizzie's. All the organizations and individuals she's linked with. All the arrangements that will need cancelling.

'Use mine whenever you need,' I remind him. 'And if I can help with anything, the school stuff, or looking after Florence when you go back to work, I can reduce my hours. Anything.'

We decide that Florence can go without a bath. I supervise her getting ready for bed and read her book, then she asks for Jack and he stays with her. Downstairs I nod off myself and come to with a start when he returns.

It is windy, a storm is forecast. In bed, I lie with the duvet tight around me and listen to the wind, to the bumping of the gate and the sudden rattle of something along the alley at the back when a stronger gust blows through.

It used to be one thing I relished, being warm and cosy inside while outside the wind prowled and roared. Reminders of ghost stories and adventure yarns. *It was a dark and stormy night.* That has changed.

I'm cold, chilled deep inside and I no longer feel safe.

Ruth

CHAPTER THIRTEEN

17 Brinks Avenue
Manchester
M19 6FX

I wake early. The storm is buffeting the house, heavy rain lashes against the window. Milky, unsettled, starts to wash himself, then freezes, cowering. He won't even come on to my lap for a stroke.

Pain in my chest again. Perhaps I need to go back to the GP. I'm fearful that it's something serious. No, 'serious' is the wrong word. Something physical, mechanical, a blockage or a clot, a leak or a tear. That my heart is broken, not just that I am heartbroken.

Florence and Jack come down together. She has woken him. Before, she used to be happy entertaining herself for a while, able to understand that Mummy and Daddy didn't want to get up before seven, but now Jack says that as soon as she's awake she rouses him.

Jack makes her cereal and goes to have a shower.

I consider whether to broach returning to school with her but decide it's best to let Jack take the lead on that. The line between supporting and interfering is very hard to see in the circumstances. But she's his daughter and he is the sole parent now, and I trust him to judge how best to handle things with her.

There's a crashing sound from outside and Florence flinches. I feel myself wince in sympathy.

Peering out of the window, I can see that the planter I fixed up has come away from the wall. And the trellis further down is loose, moving with each fresh blast.

'It's just one of Nana's pots,' I tell her. 'You want to see?'

Non-committal, she sits for a few seconds longer then comes over, and I lift her up and show her. 'See, all the soil's spilt.'

'And the flowers,' she says.

'They were old anyway. Past their best.' Verbena and lobelia from the summer.

'You're old.'

My mind does gymnastics trying to work out what hers is thinking. That I might just collapse too? If my world feels unsteady, how much more fragile must Florence's be?

'Not really,' I say. 'I'm not past my best. Fit as a fiddle, me. Fit as a flea.'

A ghost of a smile.

Jack makes some toast and I put the kettle on again.

Kay arrives, commenting about the weather and the disruption. There's been an accident on the M60 with a lorry gone over. Trees have blocked roads and some of the rail networks have been closed where the overhead lines are down.

Almost immediately her phone goes and she leaves us to take the call in the living room.

I'm mixing a banana milkshake for Florence, whizzing the fruit with milk and a spoonful of honey, when there is a knocking at the front door, just audible above the liquidizer.

Florence has her hands pointedly over her ears.

'Let Kay get it,' I say to Jack when he moves to go.

We hear voices, male, more than one. Not Tony, I can tell his voice anywhere.

I pour the frothy yellow drink into a plastic cup.

'Can I have a straw?' Florence says.

'The bits might clog it up,' I say, 'but you can try.'

The visitors come into the kitchen with Kay. Police officers. Jackets wet with raindrops.

'Mr Jack Tennyson,' one of them says.

'Yes,' Jack says, looking to see what they want.

They both hold up their ID cards. And the one who spoke, plump, fair-haired, introduces them. PC Curtis and PC Simmons.

They must have news! Have they found you? I lean against the worktop to steady myself, intent on whatever is coming next. I'm waiting, eager, poised, holding my breath. The men move further into the room past Florence to Jack at the end of the table. Then PC Curtis speaks again. 'Jack Tennyson, I am arresting you on suspicion of the murder of Lizzie Tennyson, on the twelfth of September 2009 . . .'

Shock jolts through me, stealing my breath.

Jack jumps to his feet, his face white with shock, shouting, 'No!'

Florence flies to reach him, knocking her drink over as she drops from her chair.

'. . . you do not have to say anything . . .' Jack lunges along the side of the table, knocking over a chair. PC Simmons charges after him, blocks him in. Jack wrestles, still trying to get away. But Simmons has a set of handcuffs and he grabs for Jack's arms.

PC Curtis keeps talking as he moves after Jack, '. . . but anything you do say may be given in evidence and . . .'

Jack is struggling, shouting, 'This is crazy! I didn't do it. I didn't do anything.' Lunging to try and break free. He kicks out with his legs, knocking a chair over, wrenches away but Simmons holds him fast.

Florence is screaming, 'Daddy! Daddy!' She darts under the table to her father.

My heart hammers in my chest and I feel the pain needle through it, sharp as a knife.

'. . . may harm your defence when used in court.'

They have Jack's hands behind his back. His face has gone rigid, his eyes blazing.

Florence is screaming and hitting at PC Simmons, trying to reach her father. She squeezes past him and grabs Jack's leg.

Kay calls out, 'PC Simmons, please!'

'Let her say goodbye.' My voice cuts through the mayhem. I stare at PC Simmons, the one who has cuffed him. 'Look at her, she's four years old. Let her say goodbye.'

'Do it,' says Kay.

His eyes flicker at me. Jack is still shaking his head, his face flooded with colour now.

I move round until I'm by Florence and lift her up so she's level with Jack. She throws her skinny arms around his neck, still sobbing, 'Daddy. Daddy.'

'I'll be back soon, sweetheart,' Jack says, his voice hoarse. 'Just a silly mix-up.'

I have to pull her away, use my hands to release hers, peeling her off him, and she falls silent. Suddenly there's just the uneven shake of her breath.

The men lead Jack out. The room stinks of banana and male sweat.

The truth settles on me heavy as lead, the ground is wobbly beneath my feet. I edge on to Jack's empty chair and sit Florence on my knee and stare vacantly at the walls. Outside a car starts and there's a splatter of rain on the windows behind me.

The truth pours through me like water on sand, soaking in instantly. In my belly and my guts, in my arms, my thighs, from the nape of my neck to the soles of my feet. I'm aware of Florence, her weight on my legs, one hand gripping my little finger, the heat from her body against my stomach.

The truth solidifies inside me, granite-hard yet raw as flesh, quick as lightning and deep as space. Fathomless. I taste it in the roof of my mouth, hear it in the tick of my blood, see it in Kay's eyes, in the image of Jack trying to run, in the way Lizzie's hand caught the firelight. I smell it in the stink of body odour and ripe fruit. I feel it in my scalp and my bowels and the marrow of my bones.

You are not Broderick Litton.

Not some prowler.

Not some random stranger.

You are Jack.

Jack killed Lizzie.

Jack is you.

You are Jack.

And I hate you.

Ruth

CHAPTER FOURTEEN

Saturday 19 September 2009

The rage comes next. I round on Kay as soon as I can extricate myself from Florence, lay her on the sofa and cover her with a blanket. I'm not even astonished that she goes to sleep.

'You knew!' I say. 'You fucking knew and you let me sit here, you let Florence see that! Her own father dragged off in handcuffs.' I'm close to belting her, but turn and hit the nearest thing, the shelf with cookery books, send them flying. I would tear the walls down. But still I hold myself together.

'I'm so sorry. They weren't supposed to—'

I'm not ready to hear it. Not excuses or explanations. 'That child,' I hiss at her, determined not to weep because then I will lose the ability to say my piece, 'has lost her mother and you people tear her father away like . . . like savages.'

'I'm sorry,' she says, 'I am so sorry.'

'Go. Just get out.' I can't bear her, can't bear it. 'Just get out.'

'But—'

'I don't want you here.'

'I'll ring you later.' At least she doesn't argue with me.

A band tightens around my skull and a sweet, brackish taste floods my mouth. In the garden I vomit down the drain, the rain pelting on my back and drenching my hair.

I have to see Tony.

* * *

Florence is drowsy as I transfer her to the car. There's a CD of nursery rhymes among the discs in the glove compartment and I put that on. I could walk to the salvage yard, but not in this weather, in this state, not with Florence.

I'm probably not fit to drive, but it's only five minutes.

The gates are open and I don't see any customers' vehicles in the yard. The lights are on in Tony's office. I park so that I will be able to see Florence from the windows.

It is years since I've been here but it hasn't changed much. Though I can see he's surfaced the central courtyard, which used to be rutted and pitted and prone to puddles. And the far end of the lot, once a pair of garages, is now a large open-fronted area with a roof and aisles, presumably for various categories of stock. Adjoining the office and opposite, across the yard, are the same assortment of prefabs, sheds and lean-tos where people can browse for doorknobs and candelabra, newel posts and stained-glass panels.

My hair flies about, blinding me as I cross to the office.

Tony must have heard the car, because he opens the door before I reach it. He steps back and lets me inside.

'They've arrested Jack,' I say, 'just now, at my house.' My voice is blurred, my mouth dry.

His face moves, eyes blinking, mouth working.

'For Lizzie's murder,' I say. My breath comes sharp, blades in it.

The blood falls from Tony's face, leaving him a ghastly white colour. He sways where he stands, then raises his face to the ceiling. He tries to speak but fails to find the words, just a few stuttering syllables. He swings round, then back to me. 'That's crazy. What the hell are they playing at! We should ring someone, a solicitor. Do something. We should . . . Good God! Fuck! It doesn't make sense.' His eyes are wild, he gasps for breath.

'Tony . . . I think they're right.'

78

'What? Have you taken leave of your senses? Bloody hell, Ruth.'

'Stop shouting and listen,' I say, but he doesn't.

'He thought the world of her; this is Jack we're talking about.'

'I know! But when they came, when they arrested him, he tried to run away. He was expecting it. Any normal person, if they were innocent, they'd be speechless, stunned, outraged, but it was just like he knew he'd been caught and he made this mad dash for it and they had to physically restrain him.'

The air seems to leak out of Tony. He moves slowly, stooping, around the desk to his ancient office chair with its curved back and castors on the legs and green leather seat and back.

I perch on the edge of the desk so that I have a clear view of the car.

'But what did they say?' He gives a great sigh, ragged and fast, and a spasm jolts through his frame.

'Nothing. I don't know. Kay was there, she knew they were coming.'

He raises his hands to the sides of his head. I am reminded of Florence when I made her milkshake.

'And they wouldn't do that, arrest him, unless there was good reason,' I say. My mind careers back to that night, bumping over the paltry facts I know. There was no sign of damage. No need to force entry. *A dozen blows at least.* Jack discovering the body. Jack's story of a night-time trip to the gym. 'What's the alternative? If it's not Jack? Broderick Litton crawls out of the woodwork after more than a year's gone by and Lizzie lets him in and he beats her to death and then conveniently disappears into the night before Jack gets back from his workout?'

'But Jack . . .' he whispers.

'I know. I know.' I bite down on my tears, breathing hard. 'I don't know what to do, I don't . . . What do we tell Florence?' I break down.

Tony comes and holds me, his arms strong and heavy round

my shoulders, my face pressed against his work sweater, which smells of damp wool and white spirit and wood smoke. Scents that send me back to camping, bonfires on the beach, rain on canvas, the three of us playing cards in the light from the Tilley‘ lamp. To days at the allotment, Lizzie in her dungarees with her toy wheelbarrow. Cycling to the library with Lizzie on the child seat, me helping set up the crèche where she will play with the other kids while I work. Tony collecting her from school and letting her act as sous-chef. Us stripping wallpaper and painting window frames and choosing where to put up bookshelves.

My face is damp, cold, and I ease away, wiping my cheeks and nose.

'Why?' Tony says. 'Why?'

I have no idea, so I say nothing.

'I can't believe it,' he says. 'Not Jack.'

Not Lizzie.

I think of Jack, his voice on the phone begging for help, standing at the gate, his teeth chattering in his head. Jack eating in my kitchen, sleeping in my bed and weeping in the night. Jack echoing the questions we were all asking.

'He's an actor,' I say. *He convinced me.*

'Actors don't kill people,' Tony bursts out. Which is a ridiculous statement to make. As if an occupation confers or removes the capacity to take a life.

I snort and laugh. Tony scowls and throws out a hand. 'You know what I mean. They might let him go, they might not charge him, it could be a mistake, a misunderstanding.' He is pleading.

I shrug.

'You really think they're right?'

I don't need to repeat myself; he can read it in my eyes.

'No, no,' he says, still not prepared to accept it.

The wind whistles through the keyhole, a soft moaning noise.

After a pause, he says, 'What happens now?'

'I don't know.'

'What does Kay say?'

'She's gone, I chucked her out.'

He looks disapproving.

'You weren't there,' I say. 'Tony, it was awful. Florence was screaming and trying to get to her dad and Jack tried to run. They way they handled it.' I shake my head.

When I see Florence move, her starfish palm against the car window, I go and fetch her in. She is cranky, restless, and complains that we've left Matilda at home. Tony distracts her, showing her how to wind the grandfather clock in the corner and taking her to see the bells and doorknockers in the sheds. But then she complains she's hungry.

'Chip shop chips,' I say to her.

She blinks with surprise. Chips from the shop are a rare treat. She has frozen chips sometimes at home but Lizzie tries to limit the amount of junk food, much as Tony and I did when Lizzie was small. That all went out the window when she was a teenager and would only eat pizza and Pot Noodles and other crap. I decided not to fight about it. There were more important issues. A couple of years' rebelling through food choices wouldn't do her much harm.

'Now?' Florence says.

Tony looks at the clock. 'The shop doesn't open until twelve.'

Will she last an hour? I don't think so.

'I want chips,' she begins to grizzle.

'We'll get chips as soon as the shop opens, but let's get you something now to be going on with,' I say. 'At the baker's.'

A single nod.

Tony locks up. We walk along the main road, heads bowed in the wind, past the antique and second-hand shops, to the local bakery.

Inside, Florence presses her nose against the display cabinets and surveys the sandwiches, pies and pastries, then cranes her neck, standing on tiptoe. 'Cake,' she says.

'Here.' Tony lifts her up, names the choices. Custard slice, strawberry tart, coconut macaroon, Eccles cake, chocolate fudge cake, apple pie, rocky road.

'Rocky road?' Florence says.

'It's got nuts and fruit and chocolate. Very chewy,' I say.

'Or there's fairy buns.' The assistant points them out.

Florence shakes her head.

We wait and wait as she hums and haws. Tony puts her down.

I edge her to one side so the assistant can deal with new customers. My back aches from standing still. 'Two more minutes,' I say, 'then I'll pick.'

'No!' she objects.

'We can't stand here all day.'

She seems unable to decide, rocking in an agony of indecision. I am reminded of the way she acted choosing the toy. Impatience simmers beneath my skin, my nerves already shredded by Jack's arrest. 'Get two different things,' I suggest, keeping my voice level, 'one for you and one for Matilda.'

That works.

'Rocky road for Matilda. Chocolate for me.'

We are halfway back to the yard when she bursts into tears. 'I don't want chocolate, I don't want it.'

Tony gives me a look suggesting we go back, but I think she'll just repeat it all. There's a newsagent's on the next corner and I nip in there, buy a bag of Hula Hoops and a carton of Vimto.

Florence eyes them as I come out. She is still crying. I don't say anything, but we walk on and she quietens. Once we're in Tony's office again, I open the Hula Hoops and eat a couple. Put the cakes on the table. Offer the Hula Hoops to Tony. He shakes his head until he sees me glare, then he takes one and eats it. Florence watches.

She can tell something is going on but can't quite work out what.

I shake the Vimto, pierce it with the straw and take a sip. Offer it to Florence. She takes it and drinks. All the crying will have made her thirsty.

'Can I have some of your cake?' I say.

She screws up her mouth, uncertain.

'You can have some of my Hula Hoops.'

She nods.

I give her the Hula Hoops. She eats them all. I take a morsel of cake. She eats the rest, then the Rocky Road, her little teeth cracking the nuts with relish.

Tony fields calls while we're there. There's a strange, sad intimacy in the situation. It's like we're hiding. I should speak for myself. *I'm* hiding. Playing house. Not willing to face real life. Real death.

Dead on noon, we go to buy chips, and they are huge and crisp and golden. The vinegar makes my eyes water. We eat them in the car. I burn my tongue. Florence polishes off plenty. Her appetite is amazing.

'We'd better go,' I tell Tony, 'let you get on with work.'

He shrugs. 'I don't mind.'

'We'll go.'

'If you hear anything . . .'

'Of course.'

'I'll come round later.'

I'm at sea, unmoored. I drive home, and Florence and I lie on the sofa together with Matilda and watch films back to back.

What do I do now? How on earth do I explain this to her?

Kay does ring and I am civil – just – and ask her what is happening. 'As soon as I know,' she says, 'I will tell you.'

It's not enough.

By the time night falls, the storm has gone. The trees outside are still, the ground is drying up. All is quiet. But inside me the tempest rages. I am fit to crack, like Lear. *Blow, winds, and crack your cheeks! rage! blow! You cataracts and hurricanes, spout till you have drenched our steeples, drowned the cocks!*

CHAPTER FIFTEEN

17 Brinks Avenue
Manchester
M19 6FX

Is there any chance you'll be released without charge? Just thinking of it makes me jittery. I don't want you anywhere near me, near Florence. Surely they won't let you go now; they must have hard evidence to arrest you.

You bolting, your scrabble to escape, your vehement denials – they were what betrayed you. Jumping to your feet, trying to barge past the police officer, struggling and shouting. If you were innocent, I'm sure your response would have been different. Numb disbelief, uneasy laughter, a sense of hurt, of injustice, growing anger, outrage. You should have rehearsed that better. Done the preparation. Perhaps you had, but when they came with their set faces and their handcuffs, their stolid caution learned by rote, you fluffed your lines, acted out of character, dropped the mask.

You'd done well up till then, I'll give you that. Five-star review. I had no inkling, not one iota. No moment when the thought that it might be you crept into view or tickled at the back of my skull, or niggled in my belly. No sniff of suspicion that you were anything other than a grieving husband knocked sideways by the tragedy. You were superb. Didn't put a foot wrong, not where I was concerned. Give that man an Oscar.

Ruth

CHAPTER SIXTEEN

Saturday 19 September 2009
'Where's Daddy?'

'He's had to go to work,' I lie.

Florence pulls a face. But she doesn't query the unusual way Jack left, the men who dragged him away, the fact that his hands were cuffed together and he was raging.

I resort to practicalities. 'So I'll put you to bed. Think it's time for a hairwash, too.'

'When is he coming back?'

'I don't know.'

'Soon?' she says, with a sharp nod, as if it's definite. As if by wishing it she can make it so. 'Now,' she says.

'Not now.' Though I have no idea how long Jack might be away or whether he will be back. Will I let him in? Will we sit here and drink tea and pretend he hasn't been 'helping the police with their inquiries'?

'We'll get you ready and I'll sleep back in my bed,' I say.

Her face falls in resignation, and she gives a small sigh.

The bastard. I curse him for what he has done already and the hurt that's yet to come.

Tony doesn't stay long. With Florence asleep, I'm aware that we are alone together. And that hasn't happened for years.

He looks so tired: the network of broken capillaries that craze his cheeks, a fake rosiness set against his dull eyes and the rash of grey stubble on his chin. His hand shakes when he lifts his mug of tea.

'Do you think Lizzie was seeing someone else?' he says.

I'm stung by the suggestion. 'What? No. Why would you—'

'Why would he hurt her? Why would he do that? He loved her,' Tony says, heat in the questions.

Was that it? A crime of passion? A moment's madness. Did Jack suspect Lizzie of adultery and lose his mind?

'When would she have had time?' I say. 'If she wasn't working, she had Florence. She wouldn't do that. She loved him.' There'd have been signs, surely. I'd have known, wouldn't I? But then I never knew she was pregnant.

'I need a smoke.' Tony signals to the back door.

'You started again?' It's a rhetorical question.

He goes out.

'The trellis needs mending,' he says when he comes back in.

'It's not top of my list,' I say more harshly than I meant to. Then, 'Sorry.' Tony is a doer, a problem-solver. Constructive. He wants to fix things.

He can't fix this.

The pillow on my bed smells alien, starchy, slightly cheesy. Of Jack. His tears, his sweat, his saliva. I've not the energy to change the whole bed and I don't want to wake Florence, who is asleep in the child's bed, Matilda in her hand. But I do go and fetch the pillow from the spare room and use that.

'Nana. Nana.' Florence is by the bedside, whimpering, clutching the toy kitten.

'Did you have a bad dream?' I say. *And woke up to find it was real?* 'Want a cuddle? Come on.' I edge over and throw the duvet back. She climbs in beside me and hunches up close. I put my arm around her and kiss the top of her head, which smells of my shampoo: apple and almond. I listen to her breathing. Little sips that grow quieter and quieter.

My arm gets numb and I ease it away, flexing my hand against the pins and needles.

The next thing I know Milky is on my chest, butting my chin with his head. Begging for food. Florence is still asleep.

My nightdress is damp but I'm not hot, not sweaty. I feel the bed. The sheet is cold and wet between us, and drawing back the duvet I can smell it, sharp, ammonia. Florence has wet the bed.

She shivers as I peel the sodden pyjamas off her and turn the shower on.

When she's dry and dressed, I strip the bed. The mattress is wet too, and I wonder if I have any bicarb in to wipe it with. How can one small child contain so much urine? I should buy a mattress protector, something waterproof, just in case it happens again.

And what else? There is no plan. Time stretches ahead like foreign territory, completely unfamiliar, unknown. And I am lost. I don't speak the language or know why I'm here or what I must do.

Sunday 20 September 2009
It is late afternoon, and I have been on the computer for the first time in a week and ordered a plastic mattress cover. And remade my bed. The rest of the day has trickled away. Florence is having a strop. Kicking the sofa, her face mutinous and flushed, because I have asked her to pick up some of her toys before I read her a story. I want her to stop. I've told her twice. Close to snapping, I go into the dining room and have a silent scream, balling my fists.

How long can she keep it up? Resentment makes me truculent. I want to leave her to it, cold and passive-aggressive, rather than act the mature adult and distract her or calmly discipline her. This is no good for her, cooped up. This artificial environment. The limbo we're in. She doesn't want me, she wants her mummy and daddy. I'm on my way to tell her she can help me make toast when the doorbell goes.

Is it Jack? Panic squirts through me. Briefly I consider hiding, but that seems pathetic. My mouth is dry, my legs feel weak as I open the door.

DI Ferguson and Kay. My stomach flips over as they step inside.

Nobody's smiling. There's a hiatus from the living room, then Florence resumes her kicking.

'Come in here,' I say. We go into the dining room. The sun comes in through the window and the air is full of dust motes, golden, circling.

I move a pile of old newspapers off one chair and clear coats from another, and we all sit down.

DI Ferguson speaks. 'Ruth, I've come to tell you that we have been interviewing Jack under caution, and as a result of those interviews and the evidence gathered during our inquiry, we have agreed with the Crown Prosecution Service to bring charges.'

It is hard to breathe, as though I'm in a vacuum. My ears buzz and spots dance at the edge of my vision. 'About Lizzie?'

'Yes. Jack has been charged with Lizzie's murder. I am so very sorry.'

I gasp, even though I believed him guilty from the moment of the arrest. My skin crawls.

'I realize this must be a terrible shock,' she says. 'Is there anyone you'd like me to contact?'

Lizzie, only Lizzie.

I shake my head.

'Jack will be taken to the magistrates' court in the morning; that's a formality really, to commit the case to Crown Court. We expect him to be remanded in custody until the trial.' Her voice seems to swell and shrink.

'In prison,' I say, needing to be certain, to be crystal clear.

'That's right. It could take several months to get to court. You may be called as a witness.'

I wipe my eyes. 'Did he say why? Why he did it?'

'No. He is denying any involvement.'

'Honestly?' I'd expected him to see the game was up and confess. *They always look at the husband.* He'd said that, and I'd hurried to reassure him.

Yes, they always look at the husband.

For good reason.

'He will have to enter a formal plea,' DI Ferguson says, 'but for now he's telling us he is not guilty.'

'But you can prove he did it?' I say, my mouth dry.

'Yes. In order to charge someone, we have to consider the evidence and decide whether we have a better chance of winning rather than losing. We're confident we have.'

'We could still lose?' I say. I look from DI Ferguson, the intense gleam in her eyes, to Kay's calm gaze, searching for doubt.

'We can never be certain what the outcome of a trial will be, how a jury will vote on the evidence, but we have a very strong case.'

I think of Jack confined in a small cell, damp staining the stone walls, a metal door and bedstead, a soiled blanket.

And I wish him dead.

CHAPTER SEVENTEEN

17 Brinks Avenue
Manchester
M19 6FX

It wasn't me. Not guilty.

Three years you kept that up. That monstrous lie. Three years without the grace, the humanity, the balls to take responsibility.

In childbirth, the afterpains are often as strong as those in labour. I had them when I had Lizzie, forcing me to stop whatever I was doing and breathe through the contraction until it passed. Earthquakes have aftershocks following the original devastation, continuing to tear at anything left standing, to paralyse rescue missions, to terrorize survivors.

After the trauma of Lizzie's murder, your arrest, the understanding that she died at your hand is just like that, an aftershock. And because I am already weakened by the loss, your calumny, your crime feels equally grievous.

I cannot believe she's gone.

I cannot believe you took her.

I know these facts are true, but they are as hard to grasp as the beams of sunshine streaming into my dining room.

There's a bitter taste of triumph, sour at the back of my mouth. Any inclination to punch the air or cheer or clap with relief is suffocated by the awful, senseless waste of it all.

You have ruined your own life as well as Lizzie's. God only

knows what you've done to Florence. Hear her? Still whining and kicking the furniture.

You fool, you bloody stupid fool. I wish Lizzie had never met you. I wish you'd never been born. But then I wouldn't have Florence. I'm not in any position to bargain. To trade my granddaughter for my daughter. For what you've done cannot be undone. This isn't a dress rehearsal, no press preview. The curtain has come down, the audience are long gone. The place is tacky, tawdry in the cold glare of the house lights. You are locked up. I would rain misery and terror on your head.

I want my daughter back.

Ruth

CHAPTER EIGHTEEN

17 Brinks Avenue
Manchester
M19 6FX

Your parents won't believe it. Marian calls my mobile. She's left messages on the landline but I have not responded. It's as if I'm over the limit in terms of the emotional burden I can withstand and the prospect of a conversation with her is just too much. But I see her name and answer.

'We've heard about Jack,' she says without any preliminaries. 'It's outrageous.'

The choice of words gives me pause. I'm still wondering what exactly is outrageous when she continues, 'They're obviously determined to blame it on someone rather than do their job properly and catch the real culprit. That monster Litton is still out there, he must be having a great laugh at our expense.'

'You think Jack's innocent?' I say. This is what's outrageous. I feel a wave of heat in my face and anger blossoming in my belly.

'Of course!' she explodes. 'Ruth, he would never do something like this, not in a million years. How can you even think . . . He's innocent. I know my son. It's a terrible mistake. I don't know what they're playing at, but they've got the wrong man.' She stops, and I don't say anything.

When she speaks again, she is quieter, more measured,

though I can hear high emotion trembling at the fringes of her words. 'Ruth, honestly, Jack did not hurt Lizzie. He adored her. He needs us to believe in him, to stand by him until the truth comes out.'

'No,' I say flatly.

'Ruth—'

'No. You can do what you like.'

'You can't just condemn him outright. He's—'

'It won't be up to me, will it?' I say.

'Until we know the truth . . .'

I think of Tony's reaction after your arrest, his reluctance to believe your guilt: *Have you taken leave of your senses?* How I argued that I'd seen first-hand your impulse to run away, that surge of animal energy when you were cornered. How the hard facts meant you were far more likely to be responsible than an elusive stalker or some unidentified stranger.

Perhaps Marian has to believe in you, because she is your mother. I try to twist it round, imagine Lizzie accused of violence, of murder, but fail. I have not had a son; would that would be different, bring a different perspective? So easy to blame the women, isn't it? Blame Marian for some fault in your upbringing, some problem relating to women. Or blame Lizzie for an affair, like Tony suggested, or some provocation.

Perhaps Marian dares not allow that it might be you because of the cost to her. Parents will do anything for their children, after all. Destroy evidence, invent alibis, lie under oath. Only this year there's been the Rhys Jones case. A schoolboy shot as he played out on his bike. The killer's mother lied to the police and was charged with perverting the course of justice.

'Jack has never been in trouble in his life,' Marian says. 'You're so wrong. I simply don't understand how you can choose to believe for one moment—'

'Marian, it's not something I've chosen. It's a gut feeling. As soon as they arrested him, I knew. He tried to run away.'

'That's just ridiculous.' Now she's arsey, aggressive, telling me off. 'You're just going to abandon him?'

Any restraint snaps. 'He killed my daughter! Too bloody right I'm abandoning him. I hope he rots in jail.' I hang up.

'Nana,' Florence calls out from the living room. I close my eyes for a moment, then go through to her.

She's lying on the floor, hands by her sides, eyes half open; she shuts them tight when I come in.

'Where's Florence?' I say, pretending I can't see her. She loves hide-and-seek. Though she usually picks slightly better hiding places.

'I'm here,' she says. 'Look!'

'What are you doing down there?'

'I being dead.'

Fuck! My stomach plummets. I stamp down the urge to haul her up, to tell her to stop it. A flurry of uncertainty: should I ask her more, give her a chance to talk, or explain again what dead is, what's happened to Lizzie? See if she really understands? But I'm not ready, too wound up.

'Are you now? That's sad. So you won't want any fish fingers then?'

Her eyes fly open. 'Yes!' she says.

'How many? Three?'

'Two. No, three.' She gets up and rubs her nose on her sleeve.

I will have to tell her about you, as well. She must be confused. The scene in the kitchen, her brave attempt to protect you, to keep you. My lie about you working. I need help. No doubt there is advice online from bereavement charities about explaining death to a four-year-old. But I doubt there's much about explaining that the police think Daddy did it. That Daddy killed Mummy.

She adores you.

And I will destroy that.

Ruth

95

CHAPTER NINETEEN

17 Brinks Avenue
Manchester
M19 6FX

Rebecca is here. When I open the door, she starts talking, saying if it's a bad time she can come back later, then she dissolves into tears.

I bring her in.

Rebecca is Lizzie's soul sister. They met at primary school. Rebecca has three sisters; she's the youngest. Their dad left when Rebecca was a baby. Her mum was unhappy and took it out on the children, Rebecca particularly. Looking after four children on your own is no picnic. I felt sorry for her, Samantha, but she rebuffed any moves I made to be friendly. She worked as a secretary at a private school in Sale. On several occasions when we were collecting the kids from the after-school club I heard her belittling Rebecca. I didn't have the courage to intervene directly, but when Rebecca stayed over at ours or came to play, I made a point of praising her, because she was a lovely girl.

I loved to hear the pair of them, Lizzie and Rebecca, in fits of giggles. There was never a cross word.

It wasn't so much what Samantha said – 'Oh come on, Rebecca, are you blind or just stupid?' or 'You can damn well do without or buy a new one with your pocket money, I'm sick of you' – as the very harsh tone she used that made me so uncomfortable. And it must have hurt Rebecca.

Every time Samantha came to our house, I offered her a cup of tea or coffee. She always said no. I don't think she liked me. Perhaps she sensed that I disapproved of the way she spoke to her daughter. Perhaps she hated it herself. I could relate – when Lizzie was small and bawling her head off, I felt so cross with her, unfairly, but the emotion was there all the same. Felt almost cold in my frustration. So if I'd had four kids and a job and no partner maybe I'd be mean now and again.

Lizzie hardly ever slept over at Rebecca's. She told me in later years that Samantha used to shout at Rebecca, on and on until she made her cry, which really upset Lizzie.

Rebecca will feel Lizzie's loss so keenly.

'I'm sorry,' she keeps saying, and I tell her it's all right and I'm glad she's here. When she's calmer, we sit in the living room, still awash with Florence's toys.

'The police . . .' I clear my throat. 'They've charged Jack with Lizzie's murder.'

Rebecca nods. She has glossy brown hair, cut in a bob, and striking clothes: a black and white geometric tunic, tweedy tights, Converse trainers, chunky jewellery. On anyone else it would look bizarre. Rebecca carries it off. Her fingernails are bitten to the quick.

'He hit her?' Rebecca says.

Does she need to hear the details? Like I did? The grotesque litany of injuries. *The back of Lizzie's skull was crushed with multiple fractures, the right orbital socket around the eye was fractured, as well as the nose and the right ulna . . . A dozen blows at least.*

I nod. 'They think he used the poker.' My voice catches.

'No.' She grimaces. I sense she's feeling awkward and start talking, but she interrupts me. 'No, he hit her before.' Her lip trembles. She puts her fingers to her mouth.

My face freezes. I stare at her. 'What?'

'Jack.' She bites her thumb. 'He hit Lizzie before.'

It's like I'm falling. A swoop in my stomach. I don't know what to say. 'How . . .' I begin, then, 'When?'

She blinks rapidly. 'This summer. And before that, once that I know of.'

My head feels thick, as though the blood is clotting. Foggy. As if I've been clouted hard. Stunned.

'Are you sure?'

Rebecca nods. She has tears in her eyes. 'She told me,' she says.

And not me? The betrayal scalds me. How could Lizzie hide this?

'Tell me,' I say.

'When she was pregnant with Florence, we were supposed to be going for a swim. She cried off, she said she didn't feel like it so we were going to go for a walk instead.' Rebecca sniffs. 'I called for her and I grabbed her arm, just – I don't know why, to hurry her along or something, and she yelped.' Rebecca stops and bites her lip. 'And she told me.' Her voice is thinner now.

She was pregnant then. Pregnant this time.

'She made me promise never to say anything, to anyone. She said Jack got very down about work, he'd not had anything for a while, and she'd tried to reassure him and jolly him along and he just exploded. He really didn't mean to hurt her. He was so sorry.' Rebecca looks directly at me. 'I told her to leave. To come and stay with me. Anything. She said she had warned him, afterwards, when he was all sorry and asking her to forgive him, that if he ever touched her again she would leave him and never go back. And he swore it would never happen again.'

And Lizzie believed that? I cover my face with my hands.

I think of you crying when DI Ferguson told us Lizzie was carrying twins. Imagine you hitting her, hurting her. Your face contorted with fury. Lizzie flinching to avoid the blows, crying out as you slap her, punch her in the stomach, pull her hair. Her lovely hair.

'But it did,' I say to Rebecca. 'Happen again.'

'Everything was fine for a while,' she says. 'For years.' She shrugs. 'That's what Lizzie said.' She looks at me nervously.

'Go on,' I say. Milky comes in, his tail high as he picks his way over the bits of plastic and wood from the toy box. He jumps on to the arm of the sofa beside me.

'I'd ask sometimes how things were, but she said Jack was fine, just needed to grow up a bit. Then this summer we were going to have a girls' night out together. Us and Hannah and Faith.' Other friends. 'Lizzie cancelled. Said she had a stomach bug. It just felt a bit weird. I called round the following day, just turned up. They were both there, and Florence. Jack let me in. He was very welcoming, chatty. He made us a cuppa. He stayed in the room. And Lizzie was saying she'd been sick and not to get too close and she was asking after the girls and it was all just . . . it didn't feel right, you know?'

I don't know. I didn't know.

'I couldn't say anything with him there. I didn't want to make it worse. Then I wondered if I was imagining it. She did look wiped out. But then Florence climbed on to her knee and Lizzie yelped and went white as a sheet. She was hurt. She tried to hide it, said something about sharp elbows, but she was hurt. It was all fake. I texted her after. "Are you really OK? Anything I can do?" She just fobbed me off.'

'You should have told me,' I say.

'I couldn't. I'd promised.'

'She was in danger. If we'd known—'

'I'm sorry, Ruth,' she cries. 'She was my friend and I promised.'

Oh, Lizzie, Lizzie. How could she be so stupid?

With a lurch, I realize I am blaming her. *You* hit her. *You* killed her. I cling to that. You.

'Rebecca, you must tell the police,' I say. 'If he's done this before, then—'

'I did,' she says. 'I came up yesterday, I made a statement.'

'When?'

'Yesterday afternoon.'

Before they charged you.

'I wish I'd told you,' Rebecca says miserably. 'I wish I'd told everybody, but now it's too late.' And she is weeping and hitting at her own head.

I go and catch her fists and hold them and say, 'You weren't to know. And the only person responsible for this is Jack. No one else. Not you, not Lizzie, but Jack. Yes?'

Rebecca has left. I'm angry with her. And angry with Lizzie. I rail against them both. As well as you. You bastard. I see you belting her, thumping her. Did you swear at her too? Ridicule her, humiliate her? You bully. Is this why she died? Because you were out of control? Because you used your wife as a punchbag? Because your anger was greater than your love?

Protestations crowd my mind. Lizzie wasn't stupid. She must have known you would hit her again. If she'd told me, if I'd known, then I'd have . . . *What exactly?* A cold, cruel voice butts in: *Saved her? Reported it? Got a restraining order, an injunction? Forced him to attend anger management classes?* She stopped confiding in Rebecca; would it have been any different with me?

I do believe what I told Rebecca, that you are the only person to blame, but the fact that Lizzie bore your violence and hid it from me, that she didn't ask for my help and support, makes me want to howl. Did she not trust me? Did she imagine I'd think less of her? Or interfere? Or criticize her? Was she ashamed? Ashamed of your behaviour, ashamed of her reaction, her failure to act, to walk away? In turn I am ashamed that she kept this secret from me, that dirty, ugly secret at the heart of your marriage. Ashamed that I wasn't a good enough mother.

Did you know she was pregnant? Is that another lie? You've obviously no aversion to beating a pregnant woman. You pathetic little man. That's what bullies are, aren't they? Insecure, fearful, riddled with self-loathing. And attacking others is a way of feeling bigger, stronger, of exercising power. Is there much violence in prison? I imagine you on the receiving end as the days till your trial creep by. I'd gloat, except that's not who I want to be any more. Loathing you, despising you, on and on and on, is a way of giving power to you. I'm sick of you in my head, in my teeth and my blood and my spine.

You need exorcising. Will this work? This calling to account, the search for understanding?

I do not know.

But I have nothing else.

Ruth

CHAPTER TWENTY

17 Brinks Avenue
Manchester
M19 6FX

Florence is like a limpet. She sticks so close. She must be half convinced I'll disappear next. And no wonder. Remember how she clung to your legs when they came to arrest you? How she followed you around before then? Her diligence, her attempts to hold on to the only parent she had left came to nought, and now she is to all intent and purposes an orphan.

She sleeps with me and wets the bed every night. She is with me from waking until bedtime and often finds ways to spin that out, so it can be nine or after until she is asleep.

My response to her clinginess is ambivalent. Having lost Lizzie, I want to gather Florence tight to me and never let her go. And it is true, the thought of leaving her at school and coming home alone brings anxiety spinning through me. Haven't you learnt anything? my body seems to say. You let Lizzie free, let her be independent, let her fly, and look how that turned out. The danger is that I'll smother Florence, wrap her in cotton wool and make her overdependent on me, incapable of functioning properly. This need to keep her close alternates with a hunger for some solitude, some peace, some time for me, to try and get my head round what has happened. When I am not smothering her, she is suffocating me.

I know she needs a constant, reliable, loving person with her, and that has to be me, but I find the relentlessness of it so tough. I draw solace from her presence, don't misunderstand, but there are times when I just want to bow down and weep for Lizzie. Times I want to lie in bed all day or just sit in the back yard and stare at the walls. I am so very tired, I don't know how my legs hold me up, or how I can still string a sentence together.

In the night, when my resources are at their lowest, I frighten myself thinking that my selfish need for space, for time apart, will reap ill rewards.

The sun is shining, it's unseasonably warm, hot enough to sunbathe; certainly we need the sunscreen on. I am going to tell Florence what you have done – well, what you are suspected of doing. She is outside, she has been digging the soil out of the planter – the one that fell off the wall, the morning they came for you.

Milky is sprawled on the path, soaking up the heat, one eye twitching open each time Florence bangs the trowel on the ground.

I make her a drink of juice and add a straw, take it outside.

She is hunkered down and has taken off the sunhat I've lent her, safety-pinned to fit.

'Here,' I say, 'if you're not going to wear the hat, you need more cream on.'

She shrugs.

'I'll get it,' I threaten, and she snatches the hat up and pulls it on, glowers up at me from under it. 'Good girl.'

I have rehearsed what to say with both Tony and Bea. Keep it simple. Let her respond, take my cues from that. She has not asked about you since that day. But I have found her looking under the beds and in the wardrobe, and when I ask her what she's looking for she says, 'I'm not.'

She may be looking for you, or for Lizzie. Unable to accept you've gone. Hoping that if she's good, you'll both come back. She'll go home and Bert will be there and everything will be all right again.

Florence takes the juice and has a drink. A ladybird lands on my blouse. 'Look, Florence.'

She looks, gives a nod, puts her drink down and resumes scraping the soil up.

'You know about Mummy being dead,' I say.

She hesitates, lets go of the trowel, her head bent to the ground, her face obscured by the hat.

'It is very sad,' I continue. 'Mummy won't come back. She can't come back and we miss her such a lot.'

Florence presses her hand on to the compost. Is any of this going in? Getting through to her?

'You might feel cross or lonely or sad inside. I do. And you remember the other day, the men came and Daddy went with them. Well, they think maybe Daddy hurt Mummy. He . . .' I don't want to say 'killed'. 'He made her dead, they think. So he's got to stay in a special place, called prison. He's not coming home.'

'Is he coming to Nana's?' she says, hopefully. Of course – this isn't home.

'No, he's got to stay where he is for now, until they decide if he did hurt Mummy and make her die. Do you want to say anything?'

She ignores me, uses her fingers to scatter the soil.

'Is there anything you want to know – about Mummy or Daddy?'

Still no answer.

'You were a very good girl with Mummy and Daddy, their best girl. They both love you lots and lots. We don't know why Daddy hurt Mummy so she couldn't get better, but you didn't do anything wrong. You were good. Shall we have a cuddle?'

She ignores that too, straightens up, drags the hat from her head and throws it down. She goes inside.

I feel like a failure, but what did I except? She's four. I can barely remember being four; my only memory from then is of kindergarten, of a striped smock I wore for painting.

'Nana?' she calls after a few minutes. She's in the kitchen. A wasp has fallen in her cup and is spinning round, buzzing angrily in its effort to escape. I take the whole thing outside and chuck it. She waits at the door, watches the wasp until it flies off.

'I want to go home,' she says, her lip quivering.

'I'm sorry, Florence, you can't go home, you have to stay here.'

'I want to go home with Mummy.'

'Mummy's not there. Mummy's dead. She can't go home. She can't go anywhere any more. One day we will all get together, all Mummy's family, and have a special day and say goodbye, but she won't be able to hear us, or see us, because Mummy's body doesn't work any more. It's broken.'

'The doctors could make it better,' she says.

'No, they can't.'

'Can they make Daddy better?'

'Daddy's not dead. He's alive, like me and you, but he has to go to court and the people there will decide if he hurt Mummy and made her die.' All the time I'm thinking: this is grotesque, macabre, but the websites I've consulted say the same thing: be honest, talk openly, be direct, use simple age-appropriate language.

Her face is blank, like she's hiding. I have no idea where she's gone. What she is thinking or feeling.

Did she know? Know that you sometimes battered her mother? Know that Daddy got nasty and smacked Mummy hard?

Too hard this time.

What have you done?

105

Three weeks after Lizzie's death, I am at school with Florence. Time to get her back into the routine. She does not want to be here, but she is not crying or throwing a tantrum. Just very quiet.

The friends she made before, Ben and Paige, are pleased to have her back. They keep coming up with little offerings, trying to draw her out, like Milky and his dead birds for me.

Florence barely makes eye contact. I am sitting at the table nearby. We have read four books together and then, with my thighs aching from her weight (it's a child-sized chair), I persuade her to sit in the Wendy house in the corner – decorated to represent a greengrocer's. I don't expect to leave her here today. It will be a slow process.

The only time I read these days is for Florence. My library books are well overdue. I've lost all interest, any ability to concentrate, to engage. It's like losing a sense almost.

You have been named, once you'd appeared in court; it was all over the place. They used the photo from your Spotlight entry, which must be years out of date. The children in reception are too young to understand what's happened, but those with brothers or sisters in the older classes may hear it being talked about and perhaps repeat what they hear. Children will talk, will gossip, just like adults. We can only hope that Florence's infamous status won't lead to her being taunted: *Your mummy's dead. Your daddy did it.* So tempting for a child looking for easy prey.

I cannot shake the sense of shame, prickly on my skin, hot inside. Shame because you killed her, shame that I didn't know you were a risk, that I didn't protect her. We are all tainted. Would it be easier if it had been a random attack by a stranger? I imagine so. One huge loss, not two.

Ruth

CHAPTER TWENTY-ONE

17 Brinks Avenue
Manchester
M19 6FX

The independent post-mortem for your defence has been done, the coroner has released Lizzie's body. It is December.

I touch Lizzie's hand. It feels cold and smooth and dense. And dead.

The undertaker has covered her face with a white cloth. He has dressed her in the clothes I brought. The green and blue silk tunic that she loved, those linen trousers.

It is cool in the funeral parlour; my arms bristle with goose bumps. She can't feel it. Her bare arms. And her feet. Toenails polished pink to match her fingers. The undertaker has done a manicure. Her hands. Slender fingers more like mine than Tony's, but even slimmer than mine. Longer. We used to compare her to ourselves. Allocating features and traits. His eyes, my hair, his sense of humour, my love of language, his blood group, my laugh, his teeth, my fear of heights.

Her hands, fluid and fast, making signs, symbols, flowing from one shape to another, making sense. A different language, one I couldn't use, beyond a handful of words.

She never told me about your violence, not in English or in sign language. Should I have read it? In the spaces between words, in the flicker of her eye or the incline of her head? Did she ever send me a signal that I missed?

The new truth casts shadows over everything past. So now when I remember you and her – at your wedding, at the hospital when Florence was born, posing by the Andy Goldsworthy trees on that trip we made to the Yorkshire Sculpture Park – I no longer trust the memory. I see jeopardy instead, and enmity and apprehension. Her smile to you is one of sick submission, the way she catches your hand a quest for your blessing or forgiveness. Her laughter, her kiss, an effort to please, to praise, to placate.

Those times when I made invitations: *come for tea, fancy a walk, would Florence like the panto?* And she put me off: *busy, away, already booked.* Now I don't know if that was true or if she was hiding. Hiding her wounds, hiding her shame and her failure.

I raised her, Tony and I raised her, to be her own person. We encouraged her to think she could do whatever she wanted to do, be whoever she wanted to be. That her life was hers to conduct as she saw fit. That she was as good as anyone else, as strong, as beautiful, as brave. That she should treat others as she'd like to be treated. At least I thought we had.

The travesty ripples back through the past and on into the future.

Your mother speaks to me. Same old stuff about your lily-white nature. I am tempted to confront her with your identity as a wife-beater, to ask her if she knew, if there had been whispers with your earlier girlfriends. Was it something you learned from your parents? Was Marian used to feeling the back of Alan's hand, or his foot in her ribs? Where does it come from, this violence in you?

But I hold my peace, because although I'm not familiar with how these things work, I realize that Rebecca might be a witness against you, and I don't want you to know, to have a chance to prepare for that.

Marian says you want to go to the funeral. Of course you do! It makes perfect sense, all part of the charade of wronged man, dutiful spouse.

I almost choke on my rage. *Over my dead body* springs to mind but I say, 'No way.'

'He's innocent. Even if you don't believe it, he is innocent. Until proven guilty. Lizzie's his wife. He's every right—'

'It's not going to happen. Has he thought about Florence? How that will be for her?'

'She's not going, is she?' Marian sounds disgusted.

'Yes,' I say, as firmly as I can. 'It's important for her to be able to say goodbye. And it would be catastrophic for her if Jack waltzes in, then disappears again.'

But you don't care about that, do you? There's only one person that matters in your universe, and that's you. The big I Am. If you had a shred of love for your daughter or anyone else, you wouldn't be putting us all through the mockery of a trial. You'd have been honourable enough to confess, to spare her, to spare us everything that followed.

I ring Kay, blurt out what Marian said, keen for her to reassure me.

'He's able to apply for compassionate leave, and if granted, he'll be escorted to the service, but first they will have to consider a number of factors, carry out a risk assessment. Most importantly determine if there's any risk either to Jack himself or to the public, or if there might be any issues affecting public order.'

'And if I say I'll kill him if he comes anywhere near?'

'You've every right to be upset,' Kay says. 'I know it sucks, big-time.' She doesn't believe my threat.

'What about Florence? It would be terrible for her.' I think of the day they came for you, the way she flew to you. I don't know what's in her head, what she understands of all this. Whether she will instinctively cleave to you again, delighted to have you back only to see you escorted away like before. A ghastly rerun. Or whether she will fear you now. Understand that you killed Lizzie, think perhaps that she may be next. But either way your attending will only damage her. And she's not well. She is not strong enough for further trauma.

I try and tell Kay this, and she says that she is sure Florence's well-being will be taken into account.

How will they know? I think. These people who make the decision. They've not met Florence or talked to me. They don't know what a good actor you are.

You get your way. You pollute the day with your presence. I have explained to Florence until I'm blue in the face that Daddy is coming to say goodbye too but because no one has agreed if he hurt Mummy or not he will have to go back to prison afterwards. Her face is expressionless. I search it for excitement, the dance of anticipation or the shadow of anxiety in her, but find nothing.

'Daddy won't be allowed to talk to you, or pick you up or sit with you.'

She holds up Matilda.

'You'll bring Matilda? Good plan, Batman.' The toy cat is like a security blanket and has supplanted Bert in Florence's affections. Lord knows what would happen if she lost the thing.

The authorities have decided that you pose no risk to us nor we to you. There won't be a baying mob eager to tear you limb from limb. No drive-by shooters. No gang of neighbours jockeying to land one on you, no vigilantes tooled up and blood-crazed.

I haven't seen you since your arrest. As we wait outside the crematorium in our dull black clothes and with the smell of frost in the air and the murmur of mourners all about, my energy is screwed to a point, waiting for your grand entrance.

110

Tony and Denise and I greet people; some make an effort to talk to Florence. She doesn't reply, not even to those she knows, like Rebecca or my friend Bea. Nor to the deaf friends who sign to us, 'Hello' and 'Sorry'.

We have hired an interpreter for the service, someone Lizzie worked with, so that everyone can appreciate what is said.

I force myself to look directly at you. You look the same. How can you look exactly the same, now that I know what you have done? But then what did I expect? Horns, the mark of Cain, the decrepitude of Dorian Gray's portrait? There is a prison guard either side of you, and you wear handcuffs.

Florence sees you. She's standing in front of me, I have my hands on her shoulders and I feel a jump travel through her. She moves to run to you. I squeeze gently and she remembers. And sinks back towards me. She waves. A tentative wave, not lifting her hand far, a quick, uncertain gesture. I see you blanch, a flash of pain across your face. You meet my eyes. You look sad, wretched, but my heart is hardened against you like a lump of clay in my chest, dense and cold. I don't disguise my feelings, my bitterness, my anger, but once I know you have seen it naked, I turn away. I will not look at you again.

Photographers take pictures, the cameras are weapons, firing snap after snap.

The chapel is packed. Because she was murdered? If cancer or a heart attack had claimed her, would there be so many people? Some are strangers to me. Did they know her? Are they voyeurs? Do some of these strangers feel a genuine connection to someone they never met?

We don't sing hymns. No word of God or heaven in the speeches.

We play a recording of Rodrigo's Concierto de Aranjuez; the haunting melody swells in the room, and tears prick my eyes. Rebecca talks about Lizzie, a lovely warm speech. Tony reads 'Echo', his hand trembling as he holds the paper, his voice steady. Denise wheezes as she weeps. Florence is restless, turning round and kneeling up on her seat, dropping Matilda and scrabbling on the floor to retrieve her.

The woman conducting the service is a friend of Bea's, a free-range minister for hire. She talks about the importance of celebrating life. Suddenly everything falls away from me. A swirl of cold oil in the pit of my stomach, my back tightens, panic climbs through me. *Lizzie. Lizzie. Gone.* I stare at the wooden coffin carpeted thick with flowers and know she's in there. That she is going, that she's lost to me. I fear I will faint. My grief rises like a flood. I bite my tongue to keep from crying out, to keep from screaming.

I do not speak to your parents. I don't have the wherewithal to be that generous. As long as they defend you, I cast them as the enemy.

At the hotel afterwards, where we have the reception – you have been taken back by then; no buffet and booze for you – the kindness of people is overwhelming, and I long for the afternoon to be done. To escape.

You make the late edition of the paper and the regional news. ACCUSED ATTENDS WIFE'S FUNERAL. Great shot. Sorrow writ large on your face, sharp suit, hands in irons.

It's like Lizzie is an afterthought. You're top of the bill. The main attraction.

Milky has found a mouse. He chases it around the living room. I'm so shattered I'm tempted to leave him to it, but who knows where the little creature would end up, or in what state. I wait until he's caught it again, dangling from his mouth, then grab him, force open his jaws and scoop up the mouse by the skin on its back. It weighs nothing. I feel the bones slide under its loose skin. When I throw it into the garden, keeping Milky behind me with one foot, it freezes for a moment, then streaks away. In the dark comes a snatch of song, a blackbird.

I wait, hoping it will sing again, but all I hear is the rattle of a train and the howl of a motorbike ridden too fast.

Ruth

CHAPTER TWENTY-TWO

17 Brinks Avenue
Manchester
M19 6FX

No one seems to know what will happen to the house. Whether the life insurance for the mortgage will pay out in these circumstances and you'll end up owning it outright, or whether it won't and the property will be repossessed. Kay comes round to tell me that the police have finished their work there and gives me a set of keys. 'Florence can finally get Bert,' she says.

Five months have passed. She warns me the place will be a mess. We may wish to contract a specialist cleaning company to sort it out.

A mess doesn't come anywhere close. It's a foggy January morning and the air tastes dirty, a chemical tang in it. I have come in the car and brought large bags and bin liners to fetch things for Florence. The bare-leaved trees and naked bushes look desolate, dead.

The house smells sour, I notice that as I push back the door, step over the scattering of junk mail and leaflets piled up behind it.

Blood. Everywhere. Dried black splashes on the walls, across the glass front of the stove, spread over the floor. Is that the smell? My heart stumbles, kicks and beats unevenly and all the hairs on my skin rise.

Oh Lizzie, oh my Lizzie.

Some of the laminate flooring, where she lay, has been taken up. I put my hand out to steady myself and the door jamb is gritty, sticky to the touch, and leaves a glittery dark grey residue on my hands. Some sort of mould? More of it here and there on the walls in the living room and around the kitchen diner. Fingerprint powder. Smeared everywhere. And the blood, dried and cracked, flaking on the walls.

The fear won't leave me. It grows inside me, something heavy crawling up my back, hands around my throat, making me dizzy. I drop the bags and leave the house and flee for home.

I am at your house again. Tony is with me. I did consider getting someone else in to clean up, but it's another expense when money is really tight and this is something we can do ourselves, upsetting though it is. I've tried to prepare him for what we'll find, described the blood, the scene of carnage, but he's still shaken. He freezes by the couch, then swings round and I think he will leave like I did.

'The bastard,' he says. 'That bastard.' And he kicks out, smashing his foot into a side table, which splinters apart, the lamp on it crashing to the floor. 'If he gets off, comes back . . .' Tony says.

'He won't,' I snap. It's what I fear. You evading justice, taking up the reins, reclaiming Florence. They must not let you go.

But Tony is steadfast. While he rips up the floor and loads the pieces into bags for the tip, I go upstairs and collect Florence's clothes and toys, including Bert. The unease about being in the space clings to me as I'm busy sorting through Florence's clothes. She's not grown much, so most of her things will still fit. I hope the shoes will. It's the shoes that make me cry.

Why they set me off, I've no idea. But the row of them – red ankle boots, canvas sandals, blue T-bar shoes, wellies with fish painted on – just unseats me. I allow myself to weep for a few minutes, then wash my face.

The same sparkly dark dust is all over the bathroom. There are your toiletries beside Lizzie's. I feel like a voyeur.

Looking in the mirror, I wonder about you, what you saw when you did the same. Did you check your expression here before you rang me? Distraught spouse, grief-stricken lover. Did you wash your hands? You must have done. Here or in the kitchen sink. Looking at the room downstairs, the way blood is sprayed about the walls over the sofa, you must have been covered in it. I don't recall blood on your clothes; did you change before you rang me?

What will I do with Lizzie's things? I hadn't thought of that. Bracing myself, in case there is more blood, more signs of your violence, I open the door to your bedroom. But it is bland, innocuous. Some of the surfaces glimmer with the powder. On her dressing table: earrings, make-up, perfume. I sniff the bottle. Jo Malone, the orange blossom. Downstairs I can hear the creak and snap as Tony tears at the laminate. My thoughts tangle. I go back into Florence's room and carry on.

'Ruth?'

Tony comes up, 'I'm off to the tip. You going to wait here?'

'No.' I don't want to be alone in the house. 'I'll take these back.' I lift the last pair of shoes into the top of a bin bag.

'Can't believe they'd just leave it like that,' Tony says.

'I know.'

'I'll collect the new flooring on my way back here.'

'D'you want a hand putting it down?' I offer.

'Okay. I'll ring you when I'm back again.'

'You take the keys, then,' I say.

We lay half the floor, snapping the tongue-and-groove boards into place, then it's time to collect Florence from school. I can't be late. Her anxiety soars if she thinks I'm late, if she can't see me near the front of the line of parents. Tony and I have spent most of our time talking about Florence.

My knees creak and my back is stiff when I straighten up.

'I don't trust Marian and Alan not to go for custody if Jack's convicted,' I say.

'What?' he scowls. 'You are joking. Would they? They wouldn't stand a chance, would they?'

'They are a couple, and they're better off.'

'But she hardly knows them.'

'Jack's still her legal guardian,' I say, 'and if we apply for custody, he can fight it.'

Tony grits his teeth and expels air through them. 'Bloody cheek.'

'We need some advice.'

'Social services?'

I feel a lurch at the thought of an outsider judging me, judging my capacity to be Florence's carer. But I know it's better to get some professional advice and hopefully support. Surely they'll see that the best place for her is with me.

Ruth

CHAPTER TWENTY-THREE

Monday 4 January 2010

It's good to be back at work, even though I feel light-headed and tense. Probably three-quarters of the library users know me, know about Lizzie. Some were at the funeral. Most of them now offer condolences. These range from 'I'm so sorry' and 'It's good to see you' to 'They want to bring back hanging, bloody disgrace'. Which doesn't really help me much.

I've come back part-time on earlies as agreed in my meeting with the area manager. Saturdays are difficult because Florence is at home. I plan to use my leave for the school holidays. Hopefully by summer things will be easier and she will be looked after by Tony and Denise or with her friends Ben or Paige. Ben's mother has offered several times.

'Ruth? I'm Stella.' My new supervisor, a senior library assistant come from North area. She smiles and shakes my hand. 'Sorry for your loss. I don't know how you can . . . It must be so very difficult.' She gives me a sympathetic smile, then carries on, 'My cousin's brother-in-law, his grandma was one of Harold Shipman's victims. Awful.'

I am poleaxed by her clumsy attempt at – what? Empathy, solidarity?

'If you need more time, if it all gets too much, you just say.' She nods eagerly. 'You can't rush something like this.' Flashing me another smile, her teeth whitened, almost neon. I must be twenty years older, but feel like a child, as if she'll pat me on the head any moment.

'We're thinking of shaking things up a bit,' Stella says.

I look at the display for New Year in the corner – charting the different ways it is celebrated around the world – and the books in translation in front of it for people who'd like to read about another place. Then there's the frieze we did last summer to brighten up the children's library, and the mobiles made by the Sure Start group. The new notices for the pensioners' Young At Heart group. I scan the room, see the people busy on the computers, the group of Asian men gathered around the tables, talking over the news, and it all looks good to me.

'Fine,' I say. I'll bide my time, see what she does.

'What d'you think?' Tracey says when Stella has disappeared. Tracey and I have worked together for nine years. She's great, a bit lazy perhaps, reluctant to do the shelving, which some people would get brassed off about but it doesn't really bother me. She has a tough time at home: her mother has dementia and sometimes goes walkabout but so far has been returned unscathed.

'Seems friendly enough,' I say.

Tracey arches an eyebrow.

'I've only just met her,' I add. 'Bit patronizing maybe.'

Unfortunately Stella is in work when I get an urgent call from school. Florence is distressed and they think I should come and settle her or take her home.

'I'm sorry,' I say, 'I'll have to go.' My heart pattering too fast as I pull my coat on. Small upsets mushroom these days. I've lost perspective.

'Of course,' she croons. 'Perhaps you came back too early. The little girl, she must be so—'

I cut her off. 'The block loans, can you ask Tracey?'

'I will, don't you worry about a thing.' Which would be reassuring if I didn't already know that she is taking every opportunity to question my fitness for work with Tracey, under the guise of concern. Always on about how awful I must be feeling and how it's bound to affect my competence.

I can hear Florence as soon as I get close to the building, howling sobs, her throat sounding raw. She is in the Wendy house, which is now decorated like a tropical beach hut. Pictures of palm trees and surf fixed to the walls, a table with a raffia cover. Lei garlands of flowers and whole coconuts and large shells strewn about. She is curled over on her front, hands, knees and face on the floor.

'She got upset at snack time,' Lisa says. 'I think Paige was a bit too enthusiastic about handing round the drinks and something set Florence off.'

'I'm sorry,' I say. I crawl into the Wendy house and begin talking to her. 'It's all right, Nana's here now. What a sad girl, come on, it's all right now.' Stroking down her back, easing her. Gradually her crying slows and peters out. The other children have gone outside to play. There's just Lisa tidying round.

I manage to cajole Florence out of the house and we sit on a chair.

'Coffee?' says Lisa.

I'm so grateful. I know she's got thirty kids to cater to and lesson plans and God knows what else, but she's one of those people who just makes time, makes connections. Caring, I guess.

Florence's face is red and puffy, her nose swollen and snotty, lips cracked. I wipe her nose. Offer her water, which she takes in little sips. While I drink coffee, I try to think of anything new that might have troubled her. She knows I'm back at work, but I've never been late to pick her up.

'She's not done anything like this before?' I check, though I'm sure they'd have told me. Lisa shakes her head. I've no way of knowing if this is progress or not. Certainly not good for the well-being of the other kids in the class.

'Did Paige say anything? They haven't had a falling out or

. . .' I don't like to suggest it but I wonder if somebody's bullying Florence, making comments about her mum or her dad. Or me. *Your fat old-lady nana.*

'No. Paige just took her the milkshake and Florence went into meltdown. Has she had night terrors? It reminded me of that.'

'Milkshake? Was it banana?'

'Yes. For our tropical theme. How did you know? Is she allergic to bananas?'

In a manner of speaking. Oh, Florence.

I close my eyes.

I think of Jack.

With ice in my heart.

Part Two

CHAPTER ONE

17 Brinks Avenue
Manchester
M19 6FX

The first glimpse I get of you in court comes as I am led up the steps from the witness suite. My cheeks hot and my heart skipping too fast.

You are impeccably dressed, black suit and navy tie, white shirt. Sitting quietly. No hint of bravado. If you were auditioning for the role of respectable young man you'd walk it.

I haven't been able to watch the start of the trial because I am a witness, but once I've said my piece I will be here every minute. Tony must be somewhere in the room, and Denise and Bea. But I am too nervous to search for their faces. The barrister for the prosecution is called Mr Cromer. He's big, beefy, florid, with a Devonian burr in his voice and wire-rimmed specs.

I read the oath and affirm my intention to tell the whole truth and nothing but the truth.

His first questions are straightforward – my relationship to Lizzie, where I live – then he asks me about the night itself.

'I got a text from Lizzie asking me if I could babysit the following Saturday. And I texted her to say yes.'

'What time was this?'

'Eight thirty-nine in the evening.' The time is branded on

my memory. I looked at the text over and over after she'd died. Her last communication.

'Then Jack rang me,' I say. 'He was very upset; he said someone had hurt Lizzie. He thought she was dead. I told him to call the police. I went round there. Jack was outside with Florence.'

I stroked her head, she shrugged me off.

'How did he appear?' says Mr Cromer.

'Very shocked, distraught.'

'Can you remember what he was wearing?'

'No,' I say, 'not really.'

'Were his clothes stained or marked?'

'I didn't notice anything like that.'

'Please tell us what happened next.'

I draw breath. The nerves are getting worse, not better, the tinnitus in my ears making me dizzy. 'I went into the house. Lizzie was . . .' My voice goes, a kick of grief.

Mr Cromer waits. The room is hushed. I want to flee, to run back down the steps and out of the building. I do not want to be here telling all these people about how I found my daughter. I do not want to bear witness but I manage to continue. 'Lizzie was on the floor, there was blood everywhere.' I keep talking, although tears sting my eyes. 'She wasn't moving. Then the police came in and took me outside.'

Dragging me back when every cell in my body wanted to reach her, touch her, help her.

'Thank you,' Mr Cromer says. 'In the days following, Mr Tennyson stayed at your house?'

'Yes.'

'Did he speak about that evening?'

'Yes, trying to work out what had happened, and who had hurt her. Like we all were.'

'Did Mr Tennyson tell you how he and Mrs Tennyson had spent the evening?' says Mr Cromer.

'Yes, he said they had been at home. Lizzie was watching television. He went to the gym.'

'And Florence was upstairs in bed?'

'Yes,' I say.

'Was that usual – his trip to the gym?' he says.

'Yes. They both went regularly.'

I sense your eyes on me. The dock is to my left, screened in glass. You sit there with a guard.

'Did Mr Tennyson say what time he'd set off to the gym?

'Yes, around eight thirty.'

'Mr Tennyson rang you that evening; what time was that?'

'Just before eleven.' I remember earlier: the allotments, buying fish, a world that still had Lizzie in it.

'You were present when Mr Tennyson received the details of the post-mortem on the Monday?'

'Yes.' My blood freezes at the recollection. How bewildered we were as Kay took us through the initial findings.

'How did he react?'

'Stunned and shocked, like the rest of us.'

'Who else was present?'

'Tony – he's my ex-husband, Lizzie's father – and the family liaison officer. She gave us the information.'

'And on Saturday the nineteenth of September Mr Tennyson was arrested and you were there when the police made the arrest?'

'Yes,' I say. The smell of bananas and sweat and you screaming, lunging to escape.

'How did Mr Tennyson conduct himself when the arrest warrant was served?'

'He went crazy,' I say. 'He tried to get out of the house and he was yelling and fighting the police.'

When Mr Cromer has finished thanking me, your barrister gets up. Miss Dixon is about the same height as Kay, though not so willowy. She has long brown hair in a ponytail under her wig, and a sharp face. She wears an unfortunate shade of orange lipstick that draws attention to her lips, too thin for scrutiny.

'Mrs Sutton, when Mr Tennyson called you as you described, what did you think had happened?'

'I thought . . . I don't know,' I answer. 'I couldn't imagine.'

'You couldn't imagine?'

'No. It felt unreal. It was like it was happening to someone else.'

It is hard going through it all again in public, in this formal setting. I feel so exposed, like a specimen staked out for everyone to prod at and pore over.

'And when you met Mr Tennyson outside the house, did you notice anything untoward about his appearance?'

'Like what?'

'I'm sorry, Mrs Sutton, I need you to answer the question.'

'Well, he was shocked,' I say.

'Why did you invite Mr Tennyson to stay at your house?'

'He couldn't stay at theirs; it was the obvious thing to do. For him and Florence.'

'You had no qualms about him being there?' she says.

'Not then, no.'

'At that point you had no reason to suspect that Mr Tennyson had any involvement in your daughter's death?' She gives a thin smile.

'No, that's right.'

'When did that change?'

'When he was arrested,' I say.

'When he was arrested,' she repeats. 'Before that point how would you have described your son-in-law?'

The words are soil in my mouth.

'Mrs Sutton?' she prompts me.

'Nice,' I say. Someone sniggers and my cheeks burn.

'Nice? Would you say he cared for your daughter?'

128

'Yes.'

'And for their daughter?' she says.

'Yes. He was – he seemed like a good man.' Are you gloating over there in your lightweight wool suit and your crisp white shirt?

'Had you any concerns about your daughter marrying him?'

'No,' I say. I was delighted. You both seemed so happy.

'Did the deceased ever complain to you about Mr Tennyson?'

The deceased. I hate her for that. 'No.'

'Is it fair to say they were happy?'

'Yes, but I didn't know—'

She is on me like a snake. 'Please only answer the questions put to you. How would you have described their marriage?'

'Happy.'

'A happy marriage. Did you ever witness any rows or arguments?'

'No,' I say.

'Did your daughter ever tell you about any rows or arguments?'

'No.'

'Were you shocked when Mr Tennyson was arrested?'

'Yes,' I say.

'Why were you shocked?'

'I don't know. I just was.'

'Mrs Sutton, you have just described to us what sounds like an ideal marriage. The happy young couple, a close family, then Mr Tennyson is arrested for murder. Would it be fair to say you were shocked because it was Mr Tennyson, your son-in-law, who was arrested?'

'I suppose so.'

'Had you suspected Mr Tennyson of any involvement in his wife's murder before that?' she says.

'No.'

'Had you any reason to believe he would hurt your daughter?'

'No.'

129

'Was the Mr Tennyson you knew a violent person?' Miss Dixon says.

I hesitate. 'No.'

'Had you ever seen him lose his temper?'

'No.' Each answer is bitter on my tongue. I imagine inventing anecdotes: *Yes, once I saw him yelling at Lizzie, they didn't know I was watching, he raised his hand and she flinched but he hit her anyway.*

'Can you explain why, when you knew him to be a good man, who loved your daughter, in an apparently happy marriage, when you had harboured no suspicion about him, you so suddenly, so fundamentally, changed your mind on his arrest?'

'Because he tried to run away, he acted guilty.'

Her mouth twitches and she says quickly, 'If he had not been arrested you would have continued to view him as a good man, a loyal husband, a close family member?'

'Yes, I suppose so,' I say reluctantly.

'Did you see much of your daughter?'

'A fair amount. I'd look after Florence sometimes.'

'How often would that be?' she says.

'Once a fortnight, maybe. It varied.'

'Would you say you were close, you and your daughter?'

'Yes,' I say.

'Did she ever confide in you?'

'Yes.'

'Can you give us any examples?'

I'm blank for a moment, still worried by the last few questions. The ringing in my ears making it harder to concentrate. 'She'd tell me if she was having any problems at work,' I say, 'if someone was difficult to work with. Or if Florence had been ill, things like that.'

'Did she ever speak to you about Mr Tennyson?'

'Yes, about his work, auditions he had been to, that sort of thing.'

'And about his behaviour?' Miss Dixon says.

'No,' I say.

'And Florence, how would you describe her relationship with her father?'

'Very good.'

'Mr Tennyson was Florence's main carer in recent months?'

'Yes,' I say.

'Had you any concerns about his care for his daughter?'

'No.'

'When Mr Tennyson was arrested, could you think of any reason why this loving father and husband might be suspected of killing his wife?'

'No, only that the police must know something I didn't.'

'It was out of character?'

'Yes.'

'It was hard to believe?'

'Yes.' With every answer she is using me to airbrush you, create a sheen of good old-fashioned wholesomeness. The gloss of a family man. She has trapped me into giving you a glowing reference. It makes me feel dirty, shabby, as though I have failed Lizzie, fallen short. I want to stay on the stand despite my jangled nerves and put it right, tell it like it is. What she has drawn from me is not the truth, nothing like the whole truth, but a partial truth cropped to fit the shape you need.

In the break, I find Tony and Denise. She is spitting mad too; we are an unlikely alliance. Tony just looks sickened.

I'm preoccupied as we go back in and take seats in the public gallery, going over my answers again and wondering if I could have done it any differently so as to undermine your cause.

Ruth

CHAPTER TWO

17 Brinks Avenue
Manchester
M19 6FX

The next witness is one of the police officers who came to the house. The one who spoke to me and asked me to take Florence home and surrender my clothes. He describes what he found in the house and what you said when he spoke to you. The same tale you told me.

Mr Cromer asks him to describe you. 'Mr Tennyson was wearing sweatpants, a lightweight sports top and black trainers. His clothing appeared to be clean.'

Then the pathologist is introduced. I feel the pulse jumping at the side of my neck, my stomach clenching as I steel myself for what's to come.

The man speaks quickly, in a monotonous style. He could be reciting the phone directory. No difference in the stress he puts on the words: 'I arrived at eleven thirty p.m.' is given the same flat delivery as 'The trauma to the skull was so severe the cranial sack had been ruptured and brain matter displaced.' Is it deliberate, so the drama of what he is telling us is stripped away?

The jury are given diagrams, an outline of the body, back and front, with the injuries noted. No photographs of Lizzie, though. A small mercy.

Mr Cromer takes us through the post-mortem findings. Some we have heard before, but there are many fresh items as well. And with each of these I feel a sting of shock and a shiver of anger that we have not been told. That we hear them in this place as though we have no more right than anyone else.

The pathologist describes the appearance of the body. That is hard to listen to. Then the procedures used. And the evidence recovered. 'We found skin under the fingernails of the victim's right hand.'

Mr Cromer asks him the significance of this.

'These are typical of defensive wounds. Consistent with a blow from the poker. The victim, raising her hand in a protective gesture.'

She knew. Oh God. Bending forward, I shield my face and close my eyes. She knew you were coming at her, holding the poker. She knew you were going to beat her. My heart cracks at that thought. I had clung to the possibility that she was oblivious, turning away when you first struck, knocked out with the first blow. But she knew. The terror. She died in fear. She tried to fight. She felt the snap of bones in her arm. Then what? What next? Her shoulder? Her face?

There is a little murmur in the room as the pathologist describes her pregnancy. To the side of us, in another section of the court, people are busy writing, typing on tablets, using mobile phones to text or tweet. Press, I realize, filling their column inches with juicy copy.

Your defence does not have any questions for the pathologist. We discuss it as we file out. 'They're not disputing any of that,' Tony says. 'Only who did it.'

Anxious to reach Florence as soon as possible, I get a taxi. Ben is playing on the Wii, Florence sitting on the floor watching, when his mum April lets me in.

'How's she been?'

'No trouble. Very quiet.'

I nod. School are worried. She is refusing to speak, refusing to join in with any of the rhymes or songs. Even one to one she's silent there. A nod, a shrug, a shake of the head is all she'll offer.

It didn't seem appropriate to explain to Florence where I was going. Especially as she might think that I'd see Jack and she wouldn't. Instead I told her I had meetings for work, not at the library but in town.

At bedtime she refuses to put on the pull-up nappies she's been using. There's no sign of the bedwetting stopping, and the accepted approach is to let it run its course. Which can be many years. Withholding drinks at bedtime or lifting children to wee during the night have little impact on the problem. Fed up with having to wash sheets every day, I'd resorted to buying the nappies. Is her mutiny an attempt to punish me for being absent, for not picking her up from school? I try not to let my irritation show, not to care much one way or the other, because I sense that if I make a big deal out of it, she will too and use it as a battleground.

In my dream I am paralysed, unable to move and pinned to the floor. You have your hand over my mouth and nose. The floor is wet and sticky, covered in blood. The blood is cold and I am shivering. I can't breathe, your hand on my face, a weight on my chest. Nothing works. My legs, my voice. I know I must move, that I am in terrible danger. I wake gasping and Florence cries out, 'Nana!'

'It's all right,' I tell her. Except the bed is wet. I change her clothes, and the sheets. I offer her a nappy. She shakes her head. I put a bath towel over the sheet on her side of the bed. In the morning everything is wet again and I am running out of clean sheets.

* * *

When Mr Cromer introduces the next witness, he makes a big play of this person's expertise and experience. How long has Mr Noon worked in crime-scene management? How many murder cases has he been involved with? How regularly does he retrain? What areas of crime-scene management does he specialize in? Mr Noon explains that his role is to minimize the chance of any contamination at the scene, to document and record the scene, to search and recover any evidence there. And in consultation with the senior investigating officer, to order forensic tests on potential evidence.

Mr Cromer has a habit of looking over the top of his glasses. Maybe he needs bifocals. Or perhaps, like me, his eyesight has passed the stage when those work. 'What did you find at the scene?' he says.

Mr Noon refers to a diagram of the living space, the items drawn on a floor plan. The two sofas form an L-shape, the shorter one in front of the back wall where the stairs go up to the left. This sofa faces the door and the television; the longer sofa is parallel to the kitchen-diner, facing the stove. An out-line represents Lizzie's body. 'From the blood patterns on the walls and the furniture we were able to establish where the protagonists were during the attack. When a weapon is moved after drawing blood, there will be drops of that blood flung and that trajectory can be mapped; the shape of the drops can tell us where the perpetrator stood and how they moved the weapon. This, coupled with information from the post-mortem, tells us more about the sequence of events. At this scene, we can deter-mine that the victim was between the large sofa and the wall where the log-burner is, and the attacker was between the end of that sofa and the television, closer to the entrance door.'

'Were there any signs of a struggle elsewhere in the property?'

'No, only in the living room.'

I think of the floorboards they removed.

'Please tell the court what items were sent for testing,' says Mr Cromer.

'From the scene?' Mr Noon asks.

'Yes, from the scene.'

'Fingerprints and footwear impressions,' he says, as if starting a long list.

Mr Cromer holds up a hand. 'The jury will, I think, be familiar with fingerprints and how they can be matched, but please tell us about footwear impressions.'

'Certainly. We now have the technology to be able to recover the impressions left by footwear, shoes and the like, from many surfaces, even carpet. Certainly from the type of laminate flooring found at the Tennysons'. These can then be matched to footwear.'

'Wouldn't the same brand of shoes leave the same marks?' Mr Cromer asks.

'Initially, but as soon as a piece of footwear is worn, it acquires marks, nicks or cuts in the sole. By comparing these, we can match impressions to an individual item.'

'You recovered footwear impressions from the scene?' says Mr Cromer.

'Yes. As with fingerprints, there were many sets found. Together these could tell us who had been at the house. And the footwear impressions would show traffic since the floor was last cleaned.'

I picture Florence's shoes, see her running round their living room.

'Please go on,' says Mr Cromer.

'We were able to match and discount those belonging to the deceased and to her daughter, and to match other impressions to both Mr Tennyson and Mrs Sutton.' The step I'd taken into the room before all those hands dragged me away. 'And of course we matched and eliminated footwear from officers and CSIs at the scene. We were however left with a substantial number of impressions from a pair of size ten men's running shoes which could not be accounted for. One of those impressions was close to the victim and was made in blood.'

'A bloody footprint,' says Mr Cromer.

'Shoe print,' the scientist corrects him. 'Which could only have been made during or after the attack.'

'Can you tell us any more about this shoe?'

'Yes, it was an Adidas running shoe, from the 2009 summer season,' says Mr Noon.

'Size ten?'

'That's right,' says Mr Noon.

'I'm right that clothes and footwear worn by both Mr Tennyson and Mrs Sutton were taken by the police for examination?' says Mr Cromer.

'Yes, that's common procedure.'

'And what size were the trainers that Mr Tennyson surrendered to you for comparison?' asks the barrister.

'Size ten.'

'But a different make?' says Mr Cromer.

'Yes, Nike, an older pair,' says Mr Noon.

'Were there any traces of blood on the Nike trainers?

'No.'

'And the clothes that Mr Tennyson had surrendered?'

I am a ghoul, eager to hear of blood on your garments and your shoes, to imagine you sprayed with Lizzie's blood, daubed in it, caught red-handed.

But he says no, the witness.

'Nothing?' Mr Cromer sounds incredulous.

'That's correct.'

'Was there any blood at the scene?'

'A great deal,' Mr Noon says. 'On the floor and the walls and the furniture.'

'Were you able to identify all the fingerprints?'

'Not all of them, but that is not unusual.'

'Were any fingerprints of particular interest?' Mr Cromer pushes his wire glasses up his nose.

'There were two which included blood,' says Mr Noon.

'Where were these prints?'

'There was one on the wall at the bottom of the stairs, and one on the bathroom door.'

'Did you identify these?'

'Yes, they belonged to Mr Tennyson.' There's an electric buzz of concentration in the court. It's surely damning evidence. Blood on your hands, a bloody footprint. I want to kiss Mr Cromer.

'We heard from the pathologist that a poker had been recovered from the scene and was thought to be the weapon used. Did you examine it?'

'Yes. It had been wiped clean,' says Mr Noon.

'You could tell?'

'Oh yes, otherwise we would have been able to see material from the victim on the weapon, blood, hair and so on. And fingerprints, perhaps.'

'You recovered nothing?' Mr Cromer asks.

'We did find traces of the victim's blood trapped in places where the metal was pocked or rusted and flaked, but no fingerprints. We also found an oily residue and fibres that we matched to a brand of baby wipe.'

My stomach heaves at the thought of that: the moist perfumed tissue and the bloody poker; the juxtaposition seems obscene. Someone somewhere in the forensics lab must have painstakingly tested those traces.

'Did you find such wipes at the house?' says Mr Cromer.

'Yes, there were some in the kitchen.'

'Were they visible from the living area?'

'No, they were on a shelf below the breakfast bar,' says Mr Noon.

'What else did you examine forensically?'

'We examined the contents of the ash tray from the wood-burning stove. We found synthetic material, a polyurethane, traces of a man-made substance, EVA, and rubber in the ash.'

'EVA is?' Mr Cromer says.

'Ethylene-vinyl acetate – known as foam rubber.'

'And where would that combination of material be found?'

'Most commonly in footwear and sports equipment.'

You burned your shoes! I feel pressure in my chest; Bea shoots me a look.

'Is it true to say that what you found in the ash was consistent with someone burning a pair of running shoes in the stove?' says Mr Cromer.

'Yes, it is.'

'How long would it take to reduce a pair of running shoes to ash in a stove like that?'

'About fifteen minutes if the stove was already alight.'

The warm light it cast on Lizzie's arm.

'Have you any other observations that you and the senior investigating officer felt were pertinent to the investigation?' says Mr Cromer.

'Yes, the shower in the bathroom had been used, as well as the hand basin. We detected traces of blood in the water drops on the shower screen.'

'Was the blood visible to the naked eye?'

'No, it looked like water droplets,' says Mr Noon.

You washed. You burned your shoes. Perhaps your clothes as well.

'Can you tell us about the shoes retrieved from Mr Tennyson, the Nike trainers?'

'We could match them to footwear impressions in the house. When they were examined, we found traces of soil and grit and sand and plant matter.'

'But no blood?' says Mr Cromer.

'That is correct.'

139

Miss Dixon takes each item in turn, twisting it from a damning piece of evidence into something neutral and inconclusive.

'From the analysis of blood spatter, can you tell us anything about the assailant?' Miss Dixon says. 'Height or weight, for example?'

'Only that they would have been average height – neither very tall nor very short,' says Mr Noon.

'The residue in the ash tray, were you able to say specifically where that came from?'

'No,' he says.

'Can you state categorically that it was even a pair of shoes?'

'No.'

'Were you able to determine who had used the shower at the house?' Miss Dixon says.

'No.'

'Is it possible that it was Mrs Tennyson?'

'Yes, although her hair was dry and the shower cap in the bathroom was also dry.'

'You detected blood traces in the shower, that's correct?'

'Yes.'

'Were you able to identify the blood?' says Mr Cromer.

'It was Mrs Tennyson's,' he says.

'If Mrs Tennyson had a cut on her arm or a nosebleed, could that account for the presence of blood in the shower?'

'It could,' says Mr Noon.

Lizzie did suffer from nosebleeds. Did you tell them that? Ammunition to shoot down the prosecution case?

Miss Dixon goes on, calm, methodical, relentless. 'The shoe print at the scene, the Adidas summer trainer. That's a popular brand, it was a popular design?'

'Yes, it was.'

'The top-selling style that season?' says Miss Dixon.

'Yes,' Mr Noon says.

'Thousands of pairs sold in the north-west alone?'

'That's correct.'

'You can't be certain who wore that shoe at the scene?'

'No,' says Mr Noon.

'Or who it belonged to?'

'No.'

No. No. No. All the negatives piling up, sandbags against the tide.

By the end of the session, she has eaten away at the foundations, like woodworm boring holes through the joists. So the jury see that someone wore those trainers, wielded that poker and cleaned it, but not necessarily you. The bloody footprint, the marks on the wall, the blood in the shower: they have lost their power. They no longer damn you.

I steal a glance at you, intent on finding some gleam of arrogance, a smirk tugging at your lips or cold pride in your eyes, but you are still in character. Method acting. You're good at that. But you have a great range. I saw your Richard III at the Everyman. Brutal. The transformation was spectacular.

Ruth

CHAPTER THREE

17 Brinks Avenue
Manchester
M19 6FX

Marian and Alan are here for the trial. Your staunch support-
ers. We have done no more than nod to each other coolly so far.
Today, the third day, Marian approaches me as we wait to go
through the security scanners.

'Hello,' she says. Thankfully she doesn't ask how I am – or I
might just tell her. 'We'd like to see Florence,' she says. Colour
in her face.

Tony arrives with Denise; he sends a question my way with
his eyes. *Everything OK?*

Not so as you'd notice. I give him a jaded stare.

I want to refuse Marian and Alan, don't want them anywhere near me, or Florence.

'We are her grandparents too,' Marian says when I fail to
offer any response.

'That's right,' Alan chips in.

'We could take her out,' she says.

'I don't think that's a good idea,' I say. We shuffle forward
in the queue, closer to the scanner and the guards checking the
bags of everyone entering or leaving the building.

'You can't just—' Marian almost loses her temper.

But I cut her off. 'Florence is still very clingy. She doesn't
like new situations; you'd be better seeing her at the house.'

She makes a little noise, 'Pfft!' as though she doesn't believe me, as though I am being obstructive.

'You can see for yourself,' I say bluntly. The woman ahead of me puts her bag on the tray, and when the guard signals, she goes through the security gate.

'Come round this evening,' I suggest to Marian, 'or tomorrow. She usually goes to bed at seven. Routine is important.'

The guard nods to me and I put my bag down.

'Okay,' Marian says crisply. The dislike snaps between us like static. I'm itching to throw some of the prosecution case at her. Taunt her with your missing shoes, with pristine clothes and baby wipes. But she is not the enemy, not really; you are. She just happens to be your mother, poor cow.

I pin my hopes on DI Ferguson. She must have more to tell us about the case against you.

She looks fresh and full of zest as she swears on the Bible. She describes her role much as she did when she met us.

'You supervised a series of interviews with Mr Tennyson after the murder?' says Mr Cromer.

'That's correct.'

'Can you please tell the court what Mr Tennyson's version of events was on the night in question?'

'Mr Tennyson said he and his wife had been at home, Mrs Tennyson was watching television and Mr Tennyson went to the gym. On his return, he discovered his wife on the floor in the living room. He tried to rouse her, and when that failed, he called the police, then his mother-in-law, Mrs Sutton.'

'What time did you receive the 999 call?'

'Ten fifty p.m.,' says DI Ferguson.

'Had you reason to question his account?'

'Yes. The forensic evidence did not consistently support Mr Tennyson's story.'

143

I like the word 'story'; it implies a fiction, something you made up to hoodwink us all.

'Please elaborate,' Mr Cromer says.

'Mr Tennyson stated that he tried to rouse his wife. Specifically that he approached her from the doorway, bending over to see if she was breathing. And that he shook her shoulder, her right shoulder, calling her name.' *Her ruined face, draped in blood-thick hair.* 'Had that been the case, we would expect to find traces of blood on Mr Tennyson's clothing, and certainly on his footwear, as the blood on the floor formed a pool around the deceased's head and upper body.'

'No such traces were found?'

'None.'

You cleaned up too well, that's what she's saying. In an effort to obliterate all signs of your crime, you compromised yourself. You have put your foot in it by not putting your foot in it. Priceless!

'We began to wonder if Mr Tennyson had been present at the time of the murder and had subsequently changed his clothes and footwear and concealed them. A number of items of evidence supported this scenario. The skin under Mrs Tennyson's fingernails was matched to Mr Tennyson,' says DI Ferguson.

A murmur ripples round the room, and I feel light-headed for a moment.

'Mr Tennyson had grazes on his forearm,' she goes on. 'His fingerprints in blood on the wall by the stairs and on the bathroom door showed us that Mr Tennyson had blood on his hands but not on anything he claimed to be wearing at the scene.'

'To be clear, did he have any blood on his hands when the police examined him later that night?' says Mr Cromer.

'No, he said he had washed his hands in the basin in the bathroom. We considered the presence of the victim's blood in the water droplets on the shower screen, and in addition the material from the ashes of the wood-burner, which gave us a potential explanation for the absence of the Adidas running shoes that had left an impression at the left-hand side of Mrs Tennyson's body.'

'Those shoes were never found, that's the case?' says Mr Cromer.

'That's right. However, we did find proof of purchase of a pair of those running shoes on Mr Tennyson's credit card statement from July 2009. Bought on the twenty-ninth of the month.'

My breath catches. I hear someone else gasp. Bea grabs my hand and squeezes. She has you! She has you buying the trainers. How will you wriggle out of that?

'Five weeks before the murder?' says Mr Cromer.

'That's correct.'

'Did you ask Mr Tennyson about this?' says Mr Cromer.

'The question was put to him and he said that the trainers had been an impulse buy, they had been uncomfortable, so after a couple of weeks he had taken them for recycling to the bin outside the shoe shop on Stockport Road.'

The case of the disappearing evidence. Where are we now, in some Christie novel?

DI Ferguson continues. 'We weren't able to verify this. The contents of the bag are collected every week.'

'Did anyone see Mr Tennyson on the evening of the twelfth of September?' says Mr Cromer.

'Yes, the receptionist at the gym, the clerk in the convenience store where he bought milk, and a neighbour who lives at the other end of the cul-de-sac,' DI Ferguson says.

'Did Mr Tennyson provide you with an account of the route he had taken to the gym?'

'Yes.'

'Members of the jury,' Mr Cromer says, 'you will find that mapped out for you.' It is also displayed for us on the screen.

'How long did he say it took him?'

'Mr Tennyson says it takes about half an hour to walk there?'

'What time did he claim to have left the house?'

'At half past eight,' says DI Ferguson.

'Would he pass any CCTV cameras?'

'Only here, by the bank.' She pointed to the place. 'But if he was on the far side of the street he wouldn't have been picked up by the cameras.'

Why was she saying that, giving you an excuse? I've a moment's anger, then I think perhaps she's doing it to reinforce her honesty, to show she's not trying to manipulate information, that all her cards are on the table. Leaving your side fewer points to score. DI Ferguson has nothing to hide, nothing to fear.

'Two text messages were sent from Mrs Tennyson's phone that evening, that is correct?'

'It is,' says DI Ferguson. 'One at eight thirty-eight p.m. to Jack Tennyson and one at eight thirty-nine p.m. to Ruth Sutton.'

'At which time Mr Tennyson claims he was on his way to the gym?' says Mr Cromer.

'That's right, but we believe he sent the messages before leaving the house, in an attempt to construct an alibi.'

I feel sick. Lizzie's last text, the one I've saved, treasured, is a sham, a trick.

'Did you examine Mrs Tennyson's phone?'

'We did. But we found no fingerprints on it,' says DI Ferguson.

'Is that unusual?' says Mr Cromer.

'Extremely.'

'How would you account for the lack of fingerprints?'

'The phone had been wiped clean,' she says. DI Ferguson's energy, her vitality and her self-assurance shine through. Surely this, her complete belief in the case, her detailed knowledge of how it all fits together, will persuade the jury.

'Were there any other suspicious factors that reinforced your view of Mr Tennyson as a suspect?' says Mr Cromer.

'Yes, the fact that there had been no forced entry. The fact

146

that there were no witness accounts of anyone apart from Mr Tennyson either approaching or leaving the house that evening. And no forensic evidence of another person present.'

'Though you did recover some unidentified fingerprints?' says Mr Cromer.

'Yes.'

'Could these have belonged to a prowler who was apprehended in the area and who the Tennysons had described to the police just two days before the murder?'

'No, we traced and eliminated that individual,' she says.

'And Broderick Litton, a man who had previously harassed Mrs Tennyson and made threats, did you find any evidence of him at the scene?'

'None whatsoever,' she says.

'Have you traced and eliminated him?'

'No,' DI Ferguson says, 'but I can say confidently that by the time we arrested Mr Tennyson, we no longer regarded Broderick Litton as a credible suspect. There was no evidence at all to link him to the murder.' She lays to rest all speculation about the stalker being the real killer.

'Did Mr Tennyson change his account at any point during the interviews?' says Mr Cromer.

'No.'

'Not at all?'

'No,' says DI Ferguson.

'What percentage of people are killed by strangers?' says Mr Cromer.

'A small minority; the latest figures show that only two per cent of women are killed by strangers.'

'And of those, how many would be killed by strangers in their own home?'

'I don't have figures for that, but it would be a very small number.'

'Thank you.' He gives a little bow.

* * *

Miss Dixon comes forward as Mr Cromer sits down. She will have her work cut out.

'If Mr Tennyson had been to the gym and returned as he said and found his wife, is it not possible that his clothes would be clean?'

'Not if he touched her; extremely unlikely.'

'But possible?'

'I've never seen—'

'Please answer the question, Inspector. It would be possible that he did not acquire any microscopic droplets of blood from his wife on his clothes when he returned and found her?'

'That is possible though extremely unlikely. However—'

Miss Dixon cuts her off. 'It is possible?'

'Yes.'

'Thank you.'

'You have spoken about the use of a baby wipe to clean the poker and of wipes found in the house. But you could not match the wipe used on the poker to that particular packet, could you?'

'No. Only to that brand,' says DI Ferguson.

'It is feasible that the perpetrator found the wipes when they looked for something to clean the poker with?'

'It is,' agrees DI Ferguson.

'Or that they brought wipes with them, that is feasible too?' says Miss Dixon.

'Yes,' says DI Ferguson, though you can tell she thinks it's a load of bollocks.

'And Mrs Tennyson's phone, she may well have cleaned it herself, yes?'

'She may,' says DI Ferguson.

'Had the police ever had concerns about Mr Tennyson prior to this?' says Miss Dixon?

'No.'

'He has no convictions, cautions, never been charged with a crime?' says Miss Dixon.

'That's right,' says DI Ferguson.

'And in the course of your investigation, did you establish if the deceased had reported domestic violence to the police?' says Miss Dixon.

'No, she hadn't.'

'Attended hospital with either unexplained injuries or reports of domestic violence?'

'No.'

'Sought an injunction against her husband?'

'No.'

'Raised the issue of domestic violence with her GP?'

'No.'

'Did the family inform you of any incidents of domestic violence or suspicions about domestic violence?'

'No,' says DI Ferguson.

'Your officers carried out house-to-house inquiries in the area; did any neighbours report disturbances at the Tennysons' house?'

'No.'

'Is it true that Mrs Tennyson saw a prowler in her garden on the Wednesday immediately before she was killed?' says Miss Dixon.

'Yes, but we were able to speak to that individual and rule him out of the inquiry.'

'How did you rule him out?'

'He had an alibi, which was confirmed by several independent sources. He could not have been at the house on the Saturday night.'

'An alibi,' says Miss Dixon, as though it's something she wanted to hear. 'It is true that Mrs Tennyson reported to the police that she was being stalked in 2007 and again in 2008?'

'Yes,' says DI Ferguson.

'The man was identified at that time as Broderick Litton?' Miss Dixon says.

'Yes.'

'And both Jack Tennyson and Ruth Sutton told you about this man immediately after the murder?'

'That is correct, but—'

She doesn't get the chance to finish, as Miss Dixon interrupts her. 'And you have been unable to trace and eliminate Broderick Litton?'

'We did not believe he was a credible—'

'Please answer the question,' Miss Dixon says.

'We did not trace him but we did eliminate him as a key candidate for this crime.'

'You did not trace him?'

'No,' says DI Ferguson, a hint of impatience in her tone.

'You were unable to question him about events on September the twelfth?'

'Yes.'

'So you have no alibi for Broderick Litton – a man who had hounded Mrs Tennyson and threatened her life?'

'No, but as I—'

'No further questions,' Miss Dixon says pointedly. She has managed to focus our attention away from you, from all the evidence against you, to a scapegoat, a ghost of a man, a shadowy monster.

Florence bursts into tears when I pick her up.

'She's been fine until now, honestly,' April tells me.

'What's the matter?' I ask. Florence won't talk, only cries, a raw sound that needles under my skin and jangles my nerves. 'Come on, let's get you home,' I say. I have to half drag her to the car, still bawling. Ben looks fed up with her. *Me too, pal.*

She quietens with the motion of the car, like a baby might. That's what it feels like sometimes, having an infant in the body of a four-year-old.

Once we get in, I tell her Granny and Gramps are coming to see her.

She goes very still.

'That'll be nice,' I try and encourage her.

Your trial leaves me drained physically as well as emotionally. So each evening I feel I have been through a fresh trauma, a daily car crash. Today I'm so knackered I don't bother with anything to eat except some crackers. Florence gets fish fingers again. She eats half of one and all the ketchup. What she's left I polish off. Perhaps April fed her? I didn't even ask.

Marian and Alan arrive with presents. Florence hides behind me at the door and keeps up the shy act until I pull her out by the arm. 'Come on, see what Granny's brought you.'

Florence kicks my shin, a good whack, which really hurts. I curse under my breath.

She is cranky and remains so for the whole hour they're there. She doesn't interact much at all, and it's with me when she does, which I can see is difficult for them. Marian and Alan and I have ridiculous, fragmented conversations about the traffic in Manchester and the extension to the tram network and the menu in their hotel.

As they leave, Marian tries to kiss Florence goodbye, but Florence squirms away and does her hiding-behind-me trick again.

Marian shakes her head, pulls a face at me, irritated. She thinks what? That I've coached the child? Bad-mouthed them? 'It's not you,' I say, making an effort to be diplomatic. 'She's like this with practically everyone.'

'Just a phase, then?' Marian says.

'Let's hope so,' I tell her.

Does it affect their view of you at all, of what you've done, this demonstration of the ever-growing cost? Or are they both still blinkered and gullible, driven by misplaced loyalty?

Ruth

CHAPTER FOUR

17 Brinks Avenue
Manchester
M19 6FX

Rebecca has modified her clothing; she wears a grey slubby skirt and jacket, black pumps and tights with a cream blouse. She is nervous; even when she affirms to tell the truth, her voice stutters and stalls like a dying engine.

Mr Cromer establishes how long she and Lizzie knew each other, then says, 'Miss Thornton, how would you describe your friendship?'

'We were close, best friends actually.'

'You were Lizzie Tennyson's maid of honour at their wedding?'

'Yes,' she says.

'Did you confide in each other?'

'Yes.'

'Was she happy in the marriage?'

Rebecca hesitates. 'At the beginning, yes.'

'And after?'

'Sometimes she wasn't happy,' Rebecca says.

'Do you know why?'

'Because Jack hit her.'

The words zip round the room, and half a beat later there's a swell of sound as people react. The jury members seem to lean closer, focusing greater attention on Rebecca.

And you? You swing your head, look hurt, as if this is a blow, an outrageous slander, you'd have us believe.

'Please tell us how you heard of this,' Mr Cromer says.

Rebecca relates the story of catching Lizzie in a lie, how Lizzie yelped when Rebecca touched her arm and admitted she was hurt, that she had to avoid swimming as she knew she'd have to explain the bruises.

'What was your response?' Mr Cromer says.

'I told her to get help. See if they could have some counselling or something. So it wouldn't happen again. I offered to let her stay with me if she wanted to leave.'

'Did Mrs Tennyson seek help?' says Mr Cromer.

'Not that I know of,' Rebecca says.

'Were you aware of any further incidents of domestic violence?'

'Yes.'

'When?'

'Last summer,' she says.

'Four years since the first time?'

'Yes.'

'Please tell us about it,' Mr Cromer says.

'Lizzie cancelled a get-together at the last minute, saying she'd got a stomach bug. It had been planned for ages and so the following day I called round. Jack was there and Florence. Florence climbed up on her and she yelped, she almost passed out. Jack distracted Florence. Lizzie tried to explain it away but she was in tears, in pain. She never moved from the settee all the time I was there.'

'Did you speak to her about it while you were there?' Mr Cromer says.

'I couldn't, Jack was there.'

'And afterwards did you speak to her about it?' says Mr Cromer.

'I tried, I sent her messages but she wouldn't admit there was anything wrong.'

'Did you alert anyone else at all?'

'No. I'd promised Lizzie I wouldn't the first time.' Rebecca grimaces. 'I wish I had, then she might have been all right.'

There is a flurry of objection from Miss Dixon. Rebecca is not meant to speculate like that.

The judge tells the jury to ignore the final remark.

Rebecca is crying and apologizes.

'Just a few more questions,' Mr Cromer says gently, and Rebecca nods and takes several deep breaths and wipes at her face with a large black and white polka dot handkerchief. Pure Rebecca. She nods her head, sharply, as if she's eager to continue.

'Why do you think Mrs Tennyson didn't admit you were right on the second occasion?' says Mr Cromer.

'I don't know.'

'Why would she never tell anyone else?'

'Because she was ashamed, she didn't want people to know it was happening. "I couldn't bear it", that's what she said. "I just couldn't bear it."'

'When Mrs Tennyson disclosed to you that Mr Tennyson was physically violent, were you surprised?'

'Yes,' Rebecca says.

'Why was that?' says Mr Cromer.

'I didn't think he was that type of person. I thought he was a good man and he'd treat her well.'

'Did Mrs Tennyson say anything about what had prompted the violence?'

'She said Jack had lost his temper. He was stressed because he'd not got any parts and even the auditions were drying up. She had tried to cheer him up but he took it the wrong way.'

'How did she try to cheer him up?'

'She said something would turn up and he'd have to live with being a kept man for a while.'

'Did Mrs Tennyson say how things had been between them after the attack?'

'Jack was in tears, he was so sorry; he begged her to forgive him.'

Your face is still, a sad look in your eyes. Dignified, someone else might say, stoic. Duplicitous, if you ask me.

We take apart the morning's evidence as we pick over our lunch, Tony and Denise, Bea and me. We keep revisiting the fact that you were a wife-beater, that we never knew. Still so hard to believe. The café is on one of the side streets near the law courts. There's a preponderance of legal types, dark-suited, well groomed, lugging heavy briefcases or bags and laptops about. Other people, like the four of us, are aliens to this world, swept up in it all.

Miss Dixon smiles her orange smile and begins her cross-examination. 'On the occasion in 2005 when the deceased told you about Mr Tennyson beating her, did you see any physical evidence of that?'

Rebecca doesn't answer immediately, then says, 'No.'

'No bruises or grazes, burns, anything of that nature?'

'No.'

'Did Mrs Tennyson say where Mr Tennyson had hit her, what parts of the body?'

'No.'

'Did she say how many times he had hit her?' Miss Dixon says.

A dozen blows at least.

'No,' Rebecca says.

'Did she say how long the alleged attack had lasted?'

'No.'

'So the deceased gave you absolutely no details whatsoever about the attack? Nothing at all?'

'No,' Rebecca says; she is trembling.

'Mrs Tennyson was pregnant then; how was she finding the pregnancy?'

'She was excited about it.'

'Anything else?' says Miss Dixon.

'She found it hard to sleep. I think she had bad heartburn. And she was a bit moody.'

'Moody how?'

'Just up and down with the hormones,' Rebecca says.

'So although she was excited, there were times when she felt unhappy, dissatisfied?'

'Not really.' Rebecca tries to correct the impression. 'More weepy, I think. I don't know,' she adds.

'You don't know,' the barrister echoes, and it's a horrible undermining of Rebecca. 'Miss Thornton, you were her maid of honour, her oldest friend . . . Were you pleased to see Lizzie Sutton and Jack Tennyson get married?'

'Yes.'

'You've already told the court you were surprised at her allegation of physical maltreatment. Did it occur to you that Mrs Tennyson might have been making it up?'

'No. Why would she?' Rebecca is alarmed.

'To gain sympathy?'

'She wouldn't need to do that. We were friends.'

'When did you last see Mrs Tennyson?' says Miss Dixon briskly.

'Early July last year.'

'And before that?'

'In April.'

'Three months earlier. So would it be fair to say you weren't in frequent contact any more?'

'I live in London,' Rebecca says.

'Please answer the question.'

'We texted, we spoke on the phone in between.'

'The deceased's phone records show that she contacted you a total of four times in that period,' says Miss Dixon.

'She was busy.'

'Too busy for her best friend?'

Rebecca looks wounded. I am reminded of her mother's cutting criticism and want to shield her from all this, but I am impotent.

'Did Mrs Tennyson tell you about her recent pregnancy?'

'No, she didn't,' says Rebecca.

'No, she didn't.' Miss Dixon lets the words resound with disapproval. 'She didn't confide in you about that. Isn't it fair to say that your friendship had dwindled? That you had drifted apart, that you were no longer best friends.'

'No, it's not,' Rebecca says.

'She barely bothered to keep in touch; you lived and worked two hundred miles away. You told us that Mrs Tennyson was busy, too busy to maintain her friendship, it appears to me. You're not married?' Miss Dixon says after a pause.

'No.'

'You don't have children?'

'No.'

'I put it to you that Mrs Tennyson had found all she needed in her marriage, in her child and her career. Is that not the case?'

'No . . . I don't know,' Rebecca says, muddy with misery.

'On the occasion you refer to last summer, you didn't see any physical signs of abuse, no bruises, no marks or burns?'

'No.'

'At any point since 2005 have you seen any concrete evidence of physical harm?' says Miss Dixon.

'No.'

'You assert that Mrs Tennyson spoke to you about domestic violence in 2005. When was it mentioned again?'

Rebecca falters. 'What?'

'When?'

'Never. She didn't.'

'All those months, years, and no repetition. So we might

conclude that she didn't say anything because there wasn't anything to say. Because Jack Tennyson was treating her well. Do you agree?'

'Yes,' Rebecca says in a small voice.

She's good, your barrister. Do your hopes rise each time she pulls a stunt like that? Taking something potentially damning and removing the sting from it. Reasonable doubt, that's her brief. If she produces enough of it, you will be freed.

'And the time you refer to, last summer, your interpretation was that Mrs Tennyson was in pain?'

'She was,' says Rebecca.

'But there could be other explanations for that, could there not?'

'Maybe.'

'If Florence had caught a nerve as she clambered on to her mother's lap, or even simpler, if Mrs Tennyson had a gastric complaint as she had told you, that could have been the reason, couldn't it?' says Miss Dixon.

'Yes.'

'Yet you chose to see Mrs Tennyson as a victim of marital violence as a result of your prejudice towards Mr Tennyson.'

'No,' Rebecca protests.

'Is it not true that instead of believing your friend, your best friend for many years, you leapt to far-fetched conclusions?'

'I thought—'

'You were disappointed that she hadn't joined you on your night out, and when she told you all was well, you thought she was lying? Is that the case?'

'I don't know,' Rebecca says.

'Did it occur to you that perhaps Mrs Tennyson did not want to see you, was happier spending time with her husband?'

'No.' Rebecca's face is quivering; she is close to tears.

'It's possible that Mrs Tennyson thought the friendship had run its course. Time to move on. But you couldn't accept that, so you turned up uninvited, and rather than accept her word, you invented a fantasy.'

'That's not true.'

'True?' Miss Dixon spits the word like it is toxic. 'Is it true that Mrs Tennyson said she had a stomach bug?'

'Yes, but—'

'Is it true that you turned up unannounced?'

'Yes.'

'Is it true that when you asked her afterwards by text if all was well, she said it was?'

'Yes.'

'Do you think your friend was a liar? A dishonest person?'

'No . . . yes . . . you're twisting it all up,' Rebecca says, colour flooding her face and neck.

There's an awkward pause, then Miss Dixon says, 'I realize that answering questions can be difficult at times, but a man's future, his liberty and reputation hang in the balance here and I must ensure that the jury are in full possession of the facts. I am not twisting anything, but trying to disentangle fact from fiction, sound evidence from hearsay and speculation.'

The judge stirs and says, 'A question, please, Miss Dixon.'

'Your honour.' She inclines, a little bow, then turns to Rebecca. 'Would you say Mrs Tennyson was an honest person?'

'Yes.' Rebecca is stony-faced now; her eyes barely glance off the barrister.

'You trusted what she told you?'

'Yes,' Rebecca says.

'And in the summer, she told you everything was fine, that's what you said?'

'Yes.'

'When you called unannounced to visit her, how was Mr Tennyson?'

'Charming.'

This charming man.

'He invited you in?' says Miss Dixon.

'Yes.'

'He appeared quite happy for you to talk with Mrs Tennyson?'

'Yes.'

'Made you welcome?'

What can she say but 'Yes.'

'You thought Mrs Tennyson had been assaulted, but the only basis for that was a conversation you'd had four years earlier when she made unsubstantiated allegations about Mr Tennyson. Is it fair to say you were making an assumption this time?'

'Yes,' Rebecca says coldly, her jaw rigid.

'You might have been mistaken, might you?' says Miss Dixon.

'Yes.'

'Your assumption could have been wrong, couldn't it?'

'Yes,' Rebecca says dully. She has given up.

'You never raised your concerns with anyone, did you?'

'No.'

'No,' Miss Dixon echoes, 'Did the deceased ever tell you she had reason to fear her husband, to fear for her life?'

'No,' says Rebecca.

'On the contrary, Mrs Tennyson strenuously denied all your suggestions that she had been subjected to any violence. Isn't that true?'

Rebecca glares at the lawyer but answers, 'Yes.' It's like watching someone being eviscerated. Miss Dixon is a hyena, tearing the heart and lungs, liver and lights from Rebecca's testimony.

'Did she ever tell you she loved Jack Tennyson?'

'Yes.'

'You'd lost your best friend to a new relationship, to marriage. She had committed herself to her husband. Did you feel excluded?'

'No,' Rebecca says.

'Jealous?'

'No,' she protests.

'Mrs Tennyson didn't return your calls. Perhaps you blamed Mr Tennyson for the growing distance between you?' says Miss Dixon.

'That's rubbish.' Rebecca's face glows red again.

'A simple yes or no will suffice.'

'No,' sounding churlish, almost matching the picture Miss Dixon is painting of a jealous friend out to make trouble for you, the loving husband.

'Do you not find it strange that no one, absolutely no one, not the deceased's mother or father, her other friends, her colleagues at work, her GP, not one of them ever heard any whisper of domestic violence in the relationship?'

'I don't know.'

'Do you not find it strange that you are the only person who did? And that though Mrs Tennyson allegedly,' the word sounds like a sneer, 'told you about an incident more than four years earlier, she never shared any details about it with you, not what Mr Tennyson did or where she was hurt, and you saw not one shred of physical evidence to support her allegations? Is that not strange?'

'Maybe.' Rebecca juts her chin out, and stammers, 'But it is the truth.'

Miss Dixon lets the silence stretch out so all we hear is the tremulous quality of Rebecca's final answer, then the barrister says, 'Thank you.'

By the time Rebecca leaves the witness box, the seeds of doubt are well and truly sown.

Ruth

CHAPTER FIVE

17 Brinks Avenue
Manchester
M19 6FX

The final prosecution witness is a psychologist. Mr Cromer explains that Dr Nerys Martinez is an expert witness who will be here to shed light on the area of domestic violence, which is a key part of the prosecution case.

Dr Martinez is a small, trim, dark-skinned woman; her accent has a French lilt to it.

'You have been involved in a number of studies into the phenomenon of domestic violence?' Mr Cromer says.

'Yes.'

'Isn't the violence simply a result of someone losing control of their temper?'

'Not at all. Abuse is usually planned, prepared for. The abuser has no difficulty managing his temper at work, say, or with friends.'

'In the research you have conducted, if a person has physically assaulted their spouse on one occasion, how likely is it that they will go on to do it again?'

'Extremely likely. The incidence of sole assaults that are never repeated is almost unheard of,' Dr Martinez says.

'And can you tell us why a victim of abuse might hide what was happening from close friends and family?'

'Certainly. If you'll allow me first to outline the familiar pattern of abuse and violence. Abuse is about power and control. The abuser uses threats or violence to dominate their partner. An outbreak of violence is typically followed by the abuser exhibiting guilt; he will apologize, but he will also offer excuses to explain his behaviour. Commonly a period of normality follows and the majority of victims hope that the abuser will be able to keep his promise not to do it again. This honeymoon phase is followed by the abuser fantasizing about repeating the abuse. Planning it. He will engineer a situation that creates the right circumstances for him to attack his partner. Because abuse is about power, about domination, the person on the receiving end is made to feel culpable; the abuser will accuse them of deliberately doing something to trigger the violence. The reality is that the abuser wishes to exert his domination and to do this through violence, and he will construct a situation to make that happen. In the period of regret and promises, the person suffering from the violence wishes to believe the abuser. Their self-esteem is severely undermined. They are anxious that if only they do X and Y they will be safe. They will find excuses for the behaviour of their partner. Recognizing the situation for what it is, admitting it, is a very difficult step. Asking for help even harder. So in the majority of cases the victim conceals the situation as much as they can.'

'Women will typically suffer many instances of violence before seeking help? Am I correct?' says Mr Cromer.

'That's right.'

'Would we not expect a man who does this to be a violent person in general?'

'No. Abusers choose who to abuse, and where and how, so that the abuse is hidden. They will hit the victim in places where bruises won't show. Research shows that they are capable of switching off violent behaviour if anyone else is present. The abusers are not out of control; indeed they are very much

163

in control.' This surprises me, but it helps explain how you got away with it: you focused your violence on Lizzie; none of the rest of us ever witnessed your aggression.

'And the scenario of a woman confiding in a friend that her husband has abused her, and begging her to keep it quiet, of this victim not having visible bruises or injuries, does that ring true?'

'Yes, it's very common,' says Dr Martinez.

'And explaining to her confidante that her husband had problems with work that made him short-tempered and led to his violence – that's plausible?'

'Yes, stresses around work are often given as excuses.'

'Excuses, not reasons,' says Mr Cromer.

'That's correct. The stresses are real enough but the per-petrator does not hit anyone else; only his spouse, the one person who he believes he can dominate and control and who is unlikely to report him,' says Dr Martinez.

'If we accept, for the sake of argument, that Mrs Tennyson was being violently beaten by her husband, how would you account for her silence, her denials when her friend suspected domestic violence last summer?'

'Denial and a "behind closed doors" approach is endemic with this behaviour. Lizzie Tennyson may have feared her husband and feared what would happen if she told anyone, even her close friend, about the violence. It is textbook typical behaviour of a victim in this situation. The victim is walking on eggshells.'

'If I've understood you correctly, low self-esteem, a sense of being partly responsible for the violence and feelings of shame and fear might prevent a victim from disclosing what is hap-pening to her?' says Mr Cromer.

'Yes,' she says.

'You have described to us the fact that the man can con-trol his violence and plans his attacks, but the assault on the

164

victim in this case was uncontrolled, and fatal. Isn't that a contradiction?'

'We usually see a pattern of escalation in the violence, and there are situations where the man abandons his attempts to conceal what he is doing and gives in to his desire to dominate in the most extreme way possible.'

'By taking a life?'

'That is right.'

'How many women die every year as a result of domestic violence in this country?' says Mr Cromer.

'Around a hundred.'

'Presumably, though, it is rarer among educated people, people without significant social disadvantage?' he says.

'No, that's a myth. Domestic violence affects all sectors of society, all races, all classes.'

'Is there any link between pregnancy and domestic violence?' Mr Cromer says.

'Yes. We estimate that up to thirty per cent of abuse begins in pregnancy, and it is common for abuse to get worse during pregnancy. The *British Journal of Obstetrics and Gynaecology* reports that one in six pregnant women will experience domestic violence.'

'And if the victim was seeing less of friends and family, cancelling plans, but maintained that all was well?' says Mr Cromer.

'Again consistent with the abuse. Warning signs, in fact. Withdrawal of contact with outside relationships suits the abuser; isolating the victim adds to his domination, and denial is extremely common.'

'One question.' Miss Dixon gets to her feet. 'Do people ever make false allegations of domestic violence?'

'Yes, that happens. Though it is very rare compared to the prevalence of verified allegations.'

'Why would anyone do that?' says Miss Dixon.

'There are many reasons. To attract sympathy or attention, to punish a partner, sometimes to disguise their own role as the abuser, so they can explain away any injuries acquired when they beat someone by saying they were the victim.'

You wouldn't. Surely you would not accuse Lizzie of abusing you? We don't know yet. We don't know what the props of your defence will be beyond 'It wasn't me!' and I reason that if you're claiming innocence, you will deny any prior violence.

Rebecca comes to visit that evening. She can barely sit still, so incensed is she at the experience of being mauled by your barrister. 'She made out like I was inventing it all. Because I was jealous of Jack. That is so fucking mental.' She jolts to a stop and casts a guilty glance my way. I smile and shake my head. Swearing is irrelevant.

'She made me out to be some loser, flaky, unreliable. Did the jury believe me?'

'I don't know.' I find it impossible to read those twelve faces. Not that they are expressionless; far from it. They exhibit surprise, concern, interest, repulsion and sometimes boredom. Would Lizzie have found it easier, with her expertise in non-verbal communication? Could she have told from the body language who was favouring who?

Walking on eggshells. Did she have to do that? Placate you, play nice, alert to the slightest shift in tension. How long had it been going on? From the start, before the marriage? From her first pregnancy?

'When she told you about it, did Lizzie say if it was the first time he had done it?'

'No. I assumed it was,' Rebecca says. 'I've got to go back to London tomorrow. I wish I could stay, but I can't take any more time off. If he gets away with it . . .' She chews her lip and tears spring to her eyes. 'If only I'd told someone.'

'She'd probably have denied it,' I say. Though I wish Rebecca had told me. If I'd been alerted, put it together with the fact that I was seeing less of Lizzie, could I have done anything? Were we all gradually being excluded? Were you steadily cutting the ties to make her ever more dependent on you?

'If only I'd rung her, made more of an effort,' Rebecca says. The agony of hindsight.

'You're not to blame. Not at all. Don't think like that. There's only one person in the dock. Yeah?'

She brings out the spotted hanky again. 'Yes.' Dissolving into tears.

I go and rub her back. I miss Lizzie. The physical hunger shows no sign of diminishing. Those brief embraces we had of late, one hand pressed on the shoulder, a kiss on the cheek, the tickle of her hair as we separated. The vibration of her laughter in the air.

Ruth

CHAPTER SIX

17 Brinks Avenue
Manchester
M19 6FX

Your first defence witness is another actor; there's a ripple of interest in court as people recognize him. Joshua Corridge. He's done better than you: a stint in *Emmerdale*, a regular guest actor on prime-time shows like *Spooks* and *Midsomer Murders* (how apt). He's prettier, into the bargain. He's worked on adverts, which you once told me was where the serious money was. If word gets out, there will be fans besieging the building, begging for autographs, clutching pens, baring their arms or stomachs. There's a fashion nowadays for people to get a tattoo where a name's been scrawled on their skin. Celebrity gone mad. I've never met Joshua.

'Please tell us how you know Mr Tennyson,' Miss Dixon says.

'We met at drama school, LAMDA; we became friends and ended up sharing a flat together.' His voice has a rich, syrupy tone which is perfect for selling cars and perfume.

'You've kept in touch?'

'Oh yes. We get together if I'm working here or if Jack's in London.' He looks across at you, frank, open-faced, a brief smile. Demonstrating his trust and regard.

'How would you describe Mr Tennyson?'

'A regular guy, straightforward, hard-working, a good mate.'

'Have you ever known him to be violent?'

'No.' Joshua laughs at the question. 'Never,' he adds more steadily.

'You knew Mrs Tennyson?' says Miss Dixon.

'Yes, through Jack.'

'Did you ever spend time with Lizzie and Jack Tennyson?' says Miss Dixon.

'Oh yes. Me and my fiancée. We'd make up a foursome. Not so much since Florence came along.'

'And how would you describe the relationship between Jack and Lizzie Tennyson?'

'A perfect fit,' he says. 'They loved each other, anyone could see that.'

'Did Mr Tennyson ever talk to you about any worries or concerns he had?'

'About work,' Joshua says. 'It's a tough business; most of us are out of work ninety per cent of the time. It can get you down.'

'When did Mr Tennyson discuss this with you?' Miss Dixon says.

'The last time we met, Easter last year.'

'Was Mr Tennyson depressed?'

'No, nothing like that; just a bit frustrated, but no more than anyone else would be,' Joshua says.

'Did he ever express any concerns about his marriage, or his relationship with his wife?'

'No. They were fine. She was a keeper,' he says. The phrase rings false given what happened. He hears it. 'I mean, they seemed so right for each other, they were very happy.'

The press people are busy with their phones, sending messages no doubt about the star in the witness box.

'When you heard that Mrs Tennyson had been killed, what did you do?' says Miss Dixon.

'I tried to get in touch with Jack, to tell him how sorry I was, to see if I could help in any way, but the police had his phone and it took me a while to contact him.'

'And what was your reaction when you learned he had been charged with the crime?' says Miss Dixon.

'Gobsmacked, really. It's just totally unbelievable. So far out of character. It didn't add up. Anyone who knows him will say the same.'

Then it is Mr Cromer's turn.

'You've been successful in your line of work?' Mr Cromer says.

'Yes, I've been lucky.'

'Is it just a question of luck?'

'Not just luck; you have to be good at the job, but there is an element of right place right time,' Joshua says.

'Would you say Mr Tennyson had the same talent, the same level of skill as you?'

'Yes,' Joshua says.

'What does that involve, being good at the job?'

'You have to inhabit the role, make it plausible for the audience; you have to be honest to the part, to the piece.'

'You've done theatre, like Mr Tennyson?' says Mr Cromer.

'Yes.'

'Doesn't it get wearing, night after night, repeating the lines, sustaining the role?'

'No. It's hard work, but that's what we're trained for,' says Joshua.

Miss Dixon intervenes. 'Your honour, does this have a bearing on the case?'

'Please get to the point, Mr Cromer,' the judge says.

'Your training, Mr Tennyson's training, means you would be able to repeat a performance over and over if the job required you to? Keep it convincing?'

'Yes,' Joshua says.

'Inhabit the role?'

'Yes.'

'Mr Tennyson is good at what he does?' says Mr Cromer, cleaning his glasses on a corner of his robe.

'Yes, he's very good.'

'A good actor?'

Joshua has walked straight into the trap.

There's a pause. Too long, as Joshua tries to work out a way back from this. A twitch in his jaw. Unable to think of an alternative, defeated, he says, 'Yes.'

A point scored. I'd like to clap with delight.

We get more of the same staunch sanctification from the next witness, Andy Wallington. Your best man. Unlike Joshua, he lives locally, in Bolton, so you have more regular contact.

'He was very happy,' Andy says. 'Lizzie and Florence, that was everything he wanted.' Andy is a father too; their boy is a year younger than Florence, and they have a little girl about a year old now.

'You regularly went out together, sometimes to the football?' says Miss Dixon.

'Yes.'

'City or United?'

People laugh: the club rivalry a fundamental part of the territory in Manchester.

'United,' Andy says, and gets murmurs of approval as well as groans from the opposing faction.

'Did you ever see Mr Tennyson act violently?' says Miss Dixon.

'Never.'

'Perhaps when he'd had too much to drink?'

'He could hold his drink, he wasn't an idiot,' says Andy.

'You never saw him in a fight?'

'Only breaking one up,' Andy says.

'Tell us about that.'

'It was after a night out in town. We were waiting for a cab. There was a group coming out of the club close to the taxi rank and suddenly one of them's on the floor and the others are kicking at him. Jack waded in, pulling people away, shouting that he'd called the police. That scared them off.'

'Did he tell you why he intervened?' says Miss Dixon.

'Yes. I said he was daft, they could have turned on him, and he said he couldn't stand by and see someone get beaten up.'

'And what did you think when you heard that Mr Tennyson had been charged with murder?'

'That there'd been a mistake, there must have been. Jack wouldn't do something like that in a million years.'

Mr Cromer doesn't have any questions for him. That worries me.

The third witness is the receptionist from the gym, a young woman with red hair and a cockney twang.

'You knew Mr Tennyson?' says Miss Dixon.

'Yes, he's a regular, I knew him and his wife too,' the receptionist says.

'How did he seem that Saturday evening?'

'Same as usual.'

'He wasn't preoccupied or anxious?'

'No.'

'Thank you.' Miss Dixon walks back to her seat.

As Mr Cromer gets up, he spends a moment adjusting his glasses, then says, 'How long would it take a member to sign in?'

'Not long,' the receptionist says.

'Seconds?'

'Yes.'

'So your impression of Mr Tennyson would have been fleeting?' says Mr Cromer.

'I suppose so,' she says.

'Did Mr Tennyson stop and chat?'

'No?'

'Did you speak to him?' says Mr Cromer.

'I don't think so.'

'Was he breathless?'

'I didn't notice.'

'So he may have been?' says Mr Cromer.

'Yes,' she says.

'Is it fair to say you recall very little about him from that night?'

She stalls; she knew her script before – nothing unusual – but she's unsure how to respond to the more detailed questions.

'Yes,' she says finally.

'He may well have been out of breath, nervous or on edge, but you may not have realized in that second or two. Is that so?'

'Yes.' She rolls her eyes slightly, as if she's irritated at how her turn on the stand has gone.

I imagine you there, signing in; what were you thinking? Was your heart beating too fast? Can you control things like that with your training? Can you redirect the natural impulses – to sweat, to tremble, to jitter – and settle them, control them? Just how good an actor are you?

The judge ends the day early. You will be the next witness, and he says that rather than interrupt your testimony, we will adjourn for the day.

Ruth

CHAPTER SEVEN

17 Brinks Avenue
Manchester
M19 6FX

The court feels more crowded on the day of your testimony. The atmosphere keener, edgy.

You wear the same suit, tie and fresh white shirt. Clean-shaven and well groomed, you look so ordinary. No hint of the presumed deprivations of being in prison. But not buoyant; there's a weight to the way you conduct yourself. It is probably grief, but I don't permit myself to dwell on that, to accord you that. Too bitter. And I think that if your grief were as real as mine, as savage as mine, you would not be playing charades.

Your initial replies are basic, your voice softer than I remember, but clearly articulated. You describe meeting Lizzie: 'There was a spark, straight away. I asked her out.'

'You were single at the time?' says Miss Dixon.

'No.' The smallest smile. But you are frank. 'I was with someone else but it wasn't going anywhere. I ended that and moved in with Lizzie.'

'And how would you describe your marriage?'

You start to answer, then stop, compress your lips, raise your eyes to the ceiling, obviously fighting for composure. I can feel sympathy for you, in the breath of people around me, in the glances from the jury.

My heart is hard.

'Very happy, wonderfully happy,' you say.

'Is it true that you were under pressure, with a lack of work and subsequently a reduced income?'

'Yes, that's true. But being with Lizzie, having Florence, made it bearable. And we did manage.'

'Mrs Tennyson was working full time?' says Miss Dixon.

'That's right.'

'You didn't resent the fact that she was the breadwinner?'

'No. Lizzie understood my work, she worked in theatre too. We knew it could be feast or famine. And I was happy to be the house-husband.'

'Did you know your wife was pregnant?' says Miss Dixon.

'No,' you say quietly.

'Had you discussed having more children?'

'Yes. It was something we both wanted,' you say.

'Even on one income?'

'There's never a perfect time,' you say. It's a good answer, but you evade the question.

'Mr Tennyson, you have heard Miss Thornton describe an incident in 2005 when your wife alleged that you had been physically violent. What do you say to that? Is there any truth to it?'

'None whatsoever.'

'Why would your wife make such an allegation?' says Miss Dixon.

'I really can't think. It seems so unlike Lizzie. She was always very straight, very honest. Maybe Rebecca misunderstood. That's the only thing I can think of.'

'And the second incident, last year, when Miss Thornton came to the house and believed Mrs Tennyson to be hurt?' says Miss Dixon.

'She got that wrong. Lizzie had been sick all night, she ached everywhere. The last thing you want is someone jumping on you like Florence did.'

'Mr Tennyson, did you ever hit your wife?'

Your face falls, naked pain in your eyes. 'No.' You clear your throat and repeat, 'No. Never.'

'Mr Tennyson, I want to take you through the events of the twelfth of September as they happened. You spent the day how?'

'We did the shopping in the morning, the three of us, then Lizzie went to the hairdresser in the afternoon and I took Florence to Wythenshawe Park, to the farm and the playground. Lizzie made a meal and put Florence to bed. We watched some television and I went to the gym.'

'On a Saturday night?' says Miss Dixon.

'It's a good time to go, it's not so busy,' you say.

'What time did you arrive?'

'About nine o'clock. I did my circuits, had a swim and a shower and went home. I bought some milk on the way back. Lizzie had texted me.'

'When did you get this text?'

'I didn't see it until I was at the gym, when I went to turn my phone off,' you say.

'Thank you. You returned to the house. Please tell us about that.'

'Yes. And er . . .' You frown and swallow. 'Lizzie was there on the floor, and there was a lot of blood.'

I close my eyes, the image imprinted on my mind.

'And I couldn't think, I didn't know . . . She wasn't moving. I tried to wake her. I don't think she was breathing. I didn't know if there was someone else in the house. And Florence . . .' Your voice swoops dangerously close to breaking. 'I went upstairs. Florence was asleep. There was no one there. My hands were . . . I had blood on them, I didn't want to pick her up . . .' You crumble, a fist to your forehead, eyes squeezed shut. 'I'm sorry,' you say, 'I'm sorry.' It is a bravura performance. Beside me, Bea has tears in her eyes.

You sniff loudly. Soldier on. 'I washed my hands, and then I got Florence and held her so she wouldn't see, and I went outside.' Your breathing control deserts you. Your sentences are jerky, full of kicks and stumbles. Your voice raw and thick. 'I rang the police. And then I rang Ruth. I didn't . . . I didn't know what else to do. I didn't . . .' You hide your eyes. Your shoulders work. Again you apologize.

'Liar,' I say under my breath. Heads turn. The judge looks at the gallery; he knows someone has said something. It's not dignified, perhaps. Dignity is hard to come by any more. I don't give a flying fuck for dignity.

I know what you have done.

Tony puts his hand on my arm. I behave. Suppress the urge to ridicule, to decry and undermine your performance. To give a slow hand-clap. To heckle. To boo from the gallery. Because I do not want to be chucked out and miss the next act. And the finale.

'Mr Tennyson, do you need a break?' Miss Dixon says gently.

'No,' you say. There are tissues by the dock. You dry your eyes. You take a sip of water.

'When you tried to rouse the deceased, please tell the court what you did.'

'I was calling her name and I crouched down and shook her shoulder.'

'Which shoulder?' says Miss Dixon.

'Her right one.'

'She was face down?'

'Yes,' you say.

'Parallel to the stove,' says Miss Dixon.

'Yes,' you say.

'Did you notice the poker?'

'No,' you say softly.

'You didn't touch the poker?'

'No. I never saw it, if it was there, I don't remember. All I remember is Lizzie and it was such a shock.'

'Which hand did you use to touch her shoulder?' says Miss Dixon.

'Both.'

I try and picture that. Then I remind myself that this is all claptrap. Your version to accommodate the evidence, to exonerate yourself.

'What were you wearing?' says Miss Dixon.

'A jumper, sweatpants, trainers.'

'The same items the police retained later that night?'

'Yes,' you say.

'And the Adidas running shoes you bought only five weeks before, where were they?'

'I'd given them away,' you say.

'Where?'

'To the shoe recycling on the high street.'

'Why?'

'They hurt my toes, the fit wasn't right but I couldn't return them as I'd already worn them.'

'Rather extravagant to spend ninety pounds on a pair of shoes then throw them away,' Miss Dixon says.

'Yes, it was a bad buy. I thought they'd give a little but they didn't.' I see your barrister is covering the tricky bits of your account, trying to defuse their impact before the prosecution cross-examines you.

'Can you account for the material found in the ashes from the wood-burning stove?'

'No. But Lizzie often used the stove to get rid of things. She thought it was better than landfill,' you say.

The audacity of it makes me see stars. To implicate Lizzie.

'And when the police interviewed you, what did you tell them?'

'All that I've said just now.'

'The police spoke about abrasions on your forearm and skin under the deceased's fingernails – can you explain that?' Miss Dixon says.

'Yes, she tripped when we went shopping, she grabbed at me for balance.'

'Shopping in the morning?'

'Yes,' you say.

'Thank you.' Miss Dixon takes a breath, straightens her back then says, 'Did the police ask you about anyone who might have cause to wish your wife harm?'

'Yes, and I told them about Broderick Litton. We thought that was over, there'd not been any incidents for over a year—'

She interrupts you with a raised hand. 'Mr Tennyson, please explain to us who Broderick Litton was.'

'He was stalking Lizzie,' you say.

'When did this start?'

'He saw her signing at the Octagon, back in 2006, the Christmas show. He started off like a fan. But it's a bit weird for someone to follow a sign-language interpreter like that.'

'What form did this following take?' Miss Dixon says.

'He turned up at lots of her shows, he sent her flowers. Then he invited her for dinner. She declined and he began to write to her care of the theatres. Long, rambling letters.'

'What did these letters say?'

'How much she meant to him. How she should leave me.'

'How long did this go on?' says Miss Dixon.

'About six months, then he came to the house,' you say. 'He'd somehow found out where she lived

'When was this?'

'March 2008.'

'What happened?'

'I wasn't there. Lizzie answered the door, and when she saw who it was, she just shut it again. She rang me, she was very upset.'

'And after that?'

'More letters.'

'Saying what?' says Miss Dixon.

'Same as before, but making threats, too.'

'You went to the police?'

'Yes. They said they would speak to him. They couldn't do anything else because he hadn't actually committed a crime,' you say.

'Did the harassment continue?' says Miss Dixon.

'There were a couple more letters. Very angry. Disturbing.'

'Saying what?'

'That she'd regret reporting him, that she'd be sorry. That he'd make her pay.'

'Did Mrs Tennyson keep the letters?' asks Miss Dixon.

'She gave them to the police,' you say.

'When was the last of these letters sent?'

'About two years ago. In the July. Just after her birthday. We thought he'd gone,' you say. Your eyes glitter, bright, hurt.

'In the week before Mrs Tennyson's death, on the Wednesday, there was an incident at the house?'

'Yes. Lizzie saw someone prowling in the back garden.'

'She called the police?' says Miss Dixon.

'Yes. They came round. There'd been a burglary two doors down the night before. They didn't know if it was the same person.'

'Did Mrs Tennyson ever think it might be Broderick Litton?' Miss Dixon says.

'No. She could see the man, then he ducked round the corner; she didn't get a good look at his face, but he wasn't anything like as tall as Broderick Litton.'

'Mr Tennyson, you are on oath here today, you understand that?' says Miss Dixon.

'Yes, of course.'

'And you swear to the court that you are innocent of the charges laid against you?' says Miss Dixon.

'Yes. I miss Lizzie every minute of every day. I want to clear my name.' Tears run untrammelled down your face. 'So that I can go home and look after my little girl, and the police can find out who did this terrible, terrible thing.'

'With your permission, your honour, I would like Mr Tennyson to demonstrate for the jury, using a model, how he tried to rouse his wife.'

Miss Dixon jumps up. 'Objection, your honour, theatrics have no place here.'

'This relates to the evidence?' the judge asks Mr Cromer.

'Yes, your honour, directly to the forensic evidence.'

'Objection denied.'

A dummy is brought in. Faceless, like Lizzie was by the time you'd finished with her. There's chatter while one of the ushers places it on the floor. Others lay white tape, following a diagram that Mr Cromer gives them. He explains to the jury, 'The tape represents the furniture in the room: the sofa here and the television stand, at right angles with a gap between them. These are placed exactly as they were found that night, as is the model representing the victim.'

I wonder where they got the dummy from. Is there a factory somewhere that churns them out for this sort of thing? Are they used in hospitals or research labs? Smooth, sexless, the limbs pliable, the left arm, the arm that was closest to the stove stretched out, the right arm, the broken arm, bent in place.

Mr Cromer asks you to stand beyond the tape towards where the front door would be. 'Now, Mr Tennyson, please show us how you approached and touched the body of your wife.'

You come between the taped outline of the sofa and the TV. Does this remind you of rehearsals, when you are blocking a play? Did you know you'd have to act this out?

You take two steps to reach Lizzie and crouch down, not

kneeling. Then you reach out both your hands. It looks bizarre. One hand – the left, the nearest – would make more sense.

'Was that how close you came?' asks Mr Cromer.

'I think so,' you say.

'Mr Tennyson, could you do it again, but this time remain as far away as you possibly can while still touching the right shoulder?'

You nod and retrace your steps. This time when you crouch you can only just reach; the tips of your fingers graze the smooth plastic of the dummy. Someone less agile would lose their balance. Mr Cromer asks an usher to make marks where your feet are. The usher uses chalk and draws lines by your toes and heels. You are asked to return to the witness stand.

Then Mr Cromer produces a large mat of translucent plastic, thick, flexible – like a giant mouse mat with curvy edges. There's an oval marked on one edge of it, and the usher raises the dummy and adjusts the mat beneath it so that the oval matches the outline of the head. The rest of it forms a puddle shape around the head and upper body.

'This represents the pool of blood at the murder scene,' Mr Cromer says. 'Members of the jury please note that the marks at the front of Mr Tennyson's shoes are several inches in from the edge of the pool. If Mr Tennyson had crouched there as he just demonstrated, both of his shoes would have been covered in blood. The shoes he gave the police did not have any traces of blood on them. Mr Tennyson, have you any explanation as to how this can be?'

'I must have been standing further away and then have leant right over,' you say. I can hear a frisson of anxiety in your tone.

'If you had been any further away, you would not have been able to reach, would you?' Mr Cromer says. 'I think that is obvious to everyone. Why did you use both hands?' The question is swift, and despite Mr Cromer's Devonian accent, it sounds sharp.

'It was instinctive.'

'I'd suggest to you that it would have been more straight-forward to use one hand, the left, but you needed a way of explaining the bloody fingerprints from your right hand on the stairs and the bathroom door. So you cooked up this two-handed gesture. Isn't that the case?'

'No, I used both hands,' you say.

'And washed them upstairs?'

'Yes.'

'In the sink?'

'Yes.'

'You didn't have a shower?' Mr Cromer says.

'No.'

'Then how did traces of diluted blood get in the shower cubicle?'

'Lizzie must have had a shower while I was out,' you say.

'Yet the shower cap was bone dry? And having been to the salon that day, she would not need to wash her hair again, would she?'

Her bright, bright hair.

'No.'

'I ask you again, Mr Tennyson, did you take a shower that night?' Mr Cromer paces slowly around the floor of the court-room, like a large animal circling its prey, pausing to ask each question.

'No.'

'So how did that blood get there?' says Mr Cromer.

'I don't know.'

'You don't know. Did you beat your wife?'

'No,' you say.

'Did you beat her that night?'

'No,' you say.

'Ever?'

'No.'

'But Mrs Tennyson told her friend Rebecca that you had. How do you explain that?' says Mr Cromer.

'I can't.'

'Do you think she was lying to this court?'

'No, but it wasn't true,' you say.

'Why would Rebecca lie?'

'I don't know.'

'Or do you think your wife lied when she told her friend that?'

'I don't know,' you say.

'Mrs Tennyson was pregnant the first time she spoke about you beating her. She was pregnant again last September. Did you row about that? An argument that became violent?'

'There was no argument.'

'You weren't angry? Scarcely managing on one wage and the prospect of more children, her working life disrupted and all the extra costs,' says Mr Cromer.

'I didn't know she was pregnant,' you say.

'The pathologist estimated that your wife was seven weeks pregnant; can you think of any reason why she would not have told you?'

'No, I don't know, perhaps she hadn't realized it herself.' There is no anger in your responses, which is a good way to play it. No doubt your counsel has told you to always remain polite and calm lest we glimpse your dark side.

'You claim that you left the house at eight thirty?'

'I did.'

'And you arrived at the gym at nine?' says Mr Cromer.

'Yes.'

'When did you get the text from your wife?'

'Just as I got to the gym, when I went to turn my phone off.'

'It arrived then, or had you already received it and only just noticed it?'

'It was already there,' you say.

184

'We have been told it was sent at eight-forty. Ten minutes after you claim you left home. How long does it take you to walk to the gym?'

'About half an hour,' you say.

'You don't drive there?'

'Not that distance, no.'

'You are certain you left at half past eight?'

'Yes,' you say.

'How can you be so sure?'

'*Casualty* had been on for about fifteen minutes. Lizzie liked to watch it,' you say.

Did she? I struggle to remember.

You say, 'I was thinking about watching it till the end but decided to go to the gym instead.'

'Why did you go to the gym then?'

'It's a good time to go. Quiet,' you say.

'How would you know?' says Mr Cromer, scowling, his head cocked to one side.

'Sorry?'

'How would you know it's quieter at that time?' he says slowly, and I sense something significant coming. Mr Cromer – his girth, the drawl of his accent, his steady, stately movements – might appear a little simple, but he is clever and quick-witted.

'Because people are busy Saturday nights, going out, meeting friends.'

'So you assumed it would be quieter then for that reason?' Mr Cromer says.

'Yes.' You sound slightly puzzled.

'Because you had never been to the gym on a Saturday night before, had you?'

You are stumped. For one glorious moment. Whatever you prepared for, it wasn't this. 'I don't know,' you say.

'The electronic swipe system shows members' attendance. You've never been on a Saturday after five p.m. In fact the latest you have ever been there in almost three years of membership is seven o'clock on a week night. Can you explain why your pattern of use changed so dramatically on that very night?'

'I felt like some exercise,' you say.

'I suggest you were creating an alibi, isn't that the truth of the matter?' says Mr Cromer.

'No,' you say, your face blanching and tightening, pulling your cheekbones into sharper relief.

'Yes. I put it to you that your wife was already dead when you left the house. Isn't that the case?'

'No.'

'I further suggest that before you left, you used her phone to text yourself and your mother-in-law, Ruth Sutton, to make it appear as if the victim were still alive at eight forty p.m. Then you wiped your fingerprints from the phone. Isn't that the truth?'

'No,' you say firmly.

'I also put it to you that you left the house then, at eight forty, after sending the text messages, not at eight thirty as you claim. Later exaggerating to the court how long that journey takes. How do you answer that?'

'That's not true,' you say.

'You then did your circuit training and had your swim, took your shower, and returned home, buying milk on the way, and pretended to discover your wife. Is that the real truth?'

'No.' You keep shaking your head. Your hands grip the edge of the witness stand. 'No, none of that's true.'

'Where did you dispose of your clothes, Mr Tennyson?'

'Nowhere. There weren't any other clothes,' you say.

'Why did it take you half an hour to make a fifteen-minute journey?'

'It always takes that long. It's not fifteen minutes.'

'According to calculations, if you took half an hour to cover that distance, you would have been walking at about a mile an hour, a snail's pace. You expect the members of the jury to believe that?'

'That's how long it takes,' you repeat.

'This is all a string of lies, isn't it? You'd attacked your wife before, and on September the twelfth you did it again. With fatal consequences. You took her life and then you lied about it – to the police, to Mrs Tennyson's parents, her friends. You lied and lied and denied your guilt. It's all a pack of lies, am I right?'

'No.' Your mouth is taut, lips white.

'Your account is full of holes. You did not attempt to rouse your wife. If you had have done, then your trainers, the ones you gave to the police, would have been steeped in blood. The truth is your wife was dead, you could see there was no hope, and you spent the time clearing up. You left your daughter alone in the house, with her mother dead downstairs, and went to the gym. Had you no thought for anyone but yourself?'

'I didn't do it.'

'Then how did your skin get under her fingernails as she sought to defend herself?' Mr Cromer says swiftly.

'It didn't happen like that.'

'Because it doesn't fit your fiction? Your web of deceit?'

'Because I never hurt her.' Your voice quivers. 'That's not how I got the scratches; it was when we went shopping, she tripped.'

'Do you recall what you were wearing, on that shopping trip?' says Mr Cromer.

'My grey jacket,' you say.

'This has long sleeves, am I correct?'

'Yes.'

'Can you explain to the jury how Mrs Tennyson was able to clutch at your arm and graze the skin if your arm was covered with the jacket?'

'I pushed the sleeves back, when I got warm,' you say.

187

A frankly inadequate explanation.

'Members of the jury – I am now showing you several still images taken from CCTV footage of Mr and Mrs Tennyson at Asda on the day of her death. Please note that Mr Tennyson was wearing a charcoal-grey jacket with full-length sleeves and that his sleeves are not pushed back.'

The grainy images of you and Florence and Lizzie fill my vision. No hint of the horror that is to come. Grief surges behind my breastbone.

'Can you explain why her stumble is not shown on the CCTV footage?' asks Mr Cromer.

There is a fraction of a pause, then you say, 'It happened at home, as we were unloading the car.'

I never noticed those marks. You must have been rigorous in keeping them hidden. All part of the cover-up.

'Then after you unloaded the shopping, Lizzie went to the hairdresser's, she came home and cooked a meal. That's what you said?' Mr Cromer peers at you.

'Yes.'

'Did she practise good hygiene? In the house, in the kitchen?'

'Yes,' you say.

'She would surely wash her hands in the course of cooking a meal?'

'Yes.'

'And you also claim Mrs Tennyson must have taken a shower while you were at the gym, yet you ask us to believe that the skin remained under her nails all those hours?'

'It must have done.' There's a plea in your response, asking us to believe you, but your answers are unsatisfactory, paltry.

Surely this if nothing else will convince the jury. Your flesh under her nails. I think of her hands, flashing shapes, telling stories, conveying ideas. And now, after her death, she is still signing to us, communicating the truth. *Guilty.*

'I put it to you that it didn't,' says Mr Cromer. 'There is a much simpler explanation, Mr Tennyson. As you began to beat your wife, she reached out to try and stop you. That's how you got scratched. That's how your skin got trapped under her nails.'

'No,' you say, 'no.' You swallow.

It is all so clear to me. Do they see it, the jury, do they see it like I do? You hit her arm, her head, her shoulder, her face, her head, her head, and she is forced to her knees, you hit her head, her head. She falls on to her front. You keep hitting, blood on your face, your clothes, everywhere. You move round, step in it with your right foot.

She is dead.

Exhausted, elated, panic-stricken, you see the mark your shoe has made. Take the shoes off, stick them in the stove. Grab a baby wipe, clean the poker. Strip off and pile your clothes together. Run upstairs, shower, dress. Get in character, rehearse your lines, your moves. The role of your life.

Ruth

CHAPTER EIGHT

17 Brinks Avenue
Manchester
M19 6FX

Florence hasn't eaten when I get to April's house. 'She didn't want anything. We tried pasta and she wouldn't have that. I offered her some chicken and rice but she said no.'

At home she whines that she's hungry, so I make beans on toast, cut the toast into triangles and place them around the edge of her plate, pour the beans into the middle. She throws a tantrum, bursting out with a cry so vivid I think for a moment she must have hurt herself. She wails that the bean juice is touching the toast. This sacrilege means she will not eat the toast at all, so I sling it in the compost bin.

Sobbing, she slides the beans around the plate until they're cold.

My blood chills at the thought of you leaving her in the house while you went to create your alibi. You were a good father. I thought you were. What if she had woken and gone to find her mum? It doesn't bear thinking about.

There are no more witnesses, just the closing speeches to come. Mr Cromer begins. 'On September the twelfth 2009, Lizzie Tennyson was bludgeoned to death in her living room. A shocking crime. The man in the dock, Jack Tennyson, is charged with that crime. He made strenuous attempts to conceal his actions but he made mistakes, and his account of the events of that night collapses under scrutiny. What does the evidence tell us?

'That Jack Tennyson had a history of violence towards his wife. A well-kept secret but known to Rebecca Thornton, Lizzie Tennyson's closest friend. In common with the majority of women who are victims of domestic abuse, Mrs Tennyson was unwilling or unable to ask for help, or to disclose her suffering, to reveal what was really going on in her marriage. We cannot know how frequent the abuse was, but on that night, Jack Tennyson attacked his wife again. Lizzie Tennyson tried to protect herself, reaching out, grabbing her husband's forearm, leaving scratches there and retaining some of his skin cells under her nails.

'The blows kept coming, more than twelve of them, breaking her arm, her eye socket, her shoulder, crushing her skull and ending her life. Lizzie Tennyson fell on her front alongside the stove in the living room. She suffered massive loss of blood, as you have heard from the crime-scene reports. What did Jack Tennyson do then? Repentant, did he call for help? Realizing with horror that he had destroyed the woman he loved, did he admit his guilt?' Mr Cromer pauses for effect. Looks over his glasses at the jury. 'No, he set about saving his own skin. He needed to destroy the running shoes he was wearing, one of which had left a bloody footprint close to the victim's body. He removed his running shoes and put them in the wood-burner. He fetched baby wipes from the kitchen to remove his fingerprints from the poker. He needed to get rid of the clothes he was wearing, which were all spattered with blood. He went upstairs, leaving a fingerprint on the wall and another on the bathroom door. He showered, leaving traces of blood in the stall. He dressed in clean clothes and a pair of Nike trainers.'

Mr Cromer lowers his voice, and there's a horrible intimacy

as he lays out his case. 'Jack Tennyson needed to create an alibi. He used the victim's phone to text a message to himself and another one to his mother-in-law in an attempt to make it appear as though the victim was still alive, and to imply that he had left the house. He then made his way to the gym, disposing of his bloody clothes somewhere on the way. He spent an hour and a half at the gym before leaving for home and stopping for milk at the convenience store. He then played out the charade of discovering his wife and alerting the police.'

Mr Cromer takes off his glasses and bows his head for a moment, I don't know if this is a calculated gesture or not, but it gives the impression that the weight of the case is bearing down on him. He clears his throat. 'Jack Tennyson's claim to innocence is a bare-faced lie. My learned colleague has described the defendant as a good father, a good husband, but remember, ladies and gentlemen of the jury, he is also a good actor. Trained and skilled in maintaining a false persona, able to bring all those skills to sustain a corrupt version of the events of that night. The only evidence points to Jack Tennyson. There is no unknown suspect, no other DNA on the victim's body. In a brutal attack like that, the assailant would have left material at the scene: hair, fingerprints, saliva. Lizzie Tennyson's murderer did: he left a bloody footprint, he left two fingerprints, he left traces of blood in the shower, he left skin under the victim's nails. Lizzie Tennyson's family – her daughter, her parents and friends – deserve justice. It is in your power to give them that. Put this liar, this coward, this killer behind bars where he belongs. Take into account all the evidence and find him guilty. Give them justice.'

Miss Dixon begins her summing-up with a reminder to the jury about the legal requirements of the trial. 'In his opening remarks his Honourable Justice described to you that the burden of proof is the responsibility of the prosecution. That phrase "burden of proof" is wisely chosen, because burden it is. The prosecution must convince you, the members of the jury, that Jack Tennyson is guilty beyond all reasonable doubt. And I put it to you that my learned colleague has failed miserably to make such a case. He has presented you with a hotchpotch of so-called evidence, most of which cannot withstand serious examination. Please bear with me while I review the supposed evidence against my client and demonstrate to you the legion doubts it raises.' She stops, turns away from the jury for a moment as if marshalling her thoughts, then goes on. 'Let us begin with Mr Tennyson himself and his character as testified to by witnesses at this trial. Time and again we have heard him described as honourable, likeable, responsible and, most importantly of all, a loving husband and father. A man who cared for his small daughter and supported his wife in her chosen career. Even the witnesses for the prosecution, the deceased's mother Ruth Sutton and the deceased's closest friend Rebecca Thornton, were happy to see her marry Jack Tennyson. They have referred to him, and I quote, as "a lovely man" and "a good dad".

'Asked about his relationship with Lizzie Tennyson, we have heard that Jack Tennyson loved her, he adored her, he thought the world of her. The prosecution suggests that Mr Tennyson was violent towards his wife, but I would say to you that they have failed to offer robust proof of that contention. The only evidence they have given you is uncorroborated hearsay from one person. No one else, ever . . .' she pauses for effect and raises a finger, 'ever,' she repeats, looking directly at the jury, 'heard so much as a whisper about domestic violence from the deceased or any other source. Mrs Tennyson never spoke to her GP about this, she never sought help, she never mentioned it to another friend or family. She never sought medical treatment, she never had unexplained absences from work. The issue of domestic violence is a mirage. Did Mrs Tennyson tell

Miss Thornton she'd been assaulted, or did Miss Thornton misunderstand? We will never know, but please remember that Miss Thornton saw no injuries, and when she feared that Mrs Tennyson might be at risk again, Mrs Tennyson clearly denied that she was. Why? Because it was not happening.' She emphasizes each word. 'Domestic violence was not, and never had been, an issue in this marriage. And I suggest that the thin and uncorroborated evidence of a single conversation back in 2005 is woefully inadequate.

'So what of the events of that night? The prosecution would have you believe that a loving husband and father killed his wife in a sustained and brutal attack and then set about constructing a complicated false trail to divert suspicion. This implausible scenario is not backed up by significant evidence. Just consider this.' Her voice is clear and full of serious intent, her back ramrod straight as she addresses the jury. 'There were no fingerprints on the poker to connect Mr Tennyson with the weapon used. Much has been made of missing clothes, of missing shoes, but the absence of evidence is not evidence. The forensic expert himself admitted that there was no way of proving where the deposits in the ash tray from the stove originated. And proof is crucial.' She smacks her fist on to her upturned palm.

'Without proof, there has to be doubt. Reasonable doubt. We, the defence, do not have to account for the gaps in the prosecution case; that is their job. Ours is to assess and test the evidence.

'What remains? The skin under the deceased's nails? Jack Tennyson has explained how Mrs Tennyson stumbled earlier in the day, caught at his arm for balance and grazed his skin. A simple and honest explanation. The bloody fingerprints on the wall by the stairs and the bathroom door were made as Mr Tennyson raced upstairs to check the house for intruders and rescue his little girl. The blood in the shower may well have

194

come from Mrs Tennyson herself, or even from her killer, who would have had almost two and a half hours in the house if they arrived shortly after Mr Tennyson left. Again, we the defence have no responsibility to answer those questions, but we can say that there are any number of explanations for finding blood in the shower, and the prosecution have failed resoundingly to prove a link between Mr Tennyson and that evidence. The footprint? Thousands of pairs of those shoes were sold last year in the Manchester area. It was the most popular style of the season. The prosecution have failed to prove beyond all reasonable doubt that the shoe that made that print belonged to or was worn by Mr Tennyson.'

I think of the receipt, how important it seemed. Wouldn't common sense tell the jury that the footprint was from your trainers, that you'd burnt them?

'From the moment that Mr Tennyson found his beloved wife, he has co-operated with the police and he has never wavered one iota from the account he gave at the outset. His statements have been consistent, time and again. Because he is telling the truth.' She presses her lips together, the line of garish orange forming a rueful smile.

'In the depth of his grief, and following the trauma of his wife's murder, Mr Tennyson, finding himself under the insidious cloud of suspicion, has conducted himself with unimaginable dignity. He did not murder Lizzie Tennyson. He did not attack Lizzie Tennyson. He loved her, he needs to grieve for her.' Her voice seems to fill the chamber, clear and precise. 'If you have the slightest, slenderest doubt about the evidence against him, then you will see him acquitted without stain upon his character, free to provide a loving home for his child. When you are deliberating, ask yourselves this: where is the proof? Hard, incontrovertible proof. Where? Not in the cheap theatrics of Mr Cromer's exercise with dummies. Not in the absence of blood, or the absence of clothes, or the absence of fingerprints or the absence of a pair of ill-fitting running shoes. Not in the absence of motive. I'd add another absence here – the absence of guilt.

'Mr Tennyson loved his wife. He went to the gym on that fateful night, bought milk after Mrs Tennyson texted him to ask him to bring some home, and returned to find utter devastation. Those are the hard facts, corroborated facts. Our sympathy goes to the deceased's parents and her daughter, to her friends and colleagues for this terrible, terrible crime. But it goes to Mr Tennyson too.' She speaks quietly now, drawing everyone in. 'He has lost his wife, his life partner, the mother of his child. Mr Tennyson did not commit this crime. Please study the evidence closely and it will tell you that he is an innocent man, wrongly accused, who is at your mercy. Thank you.'

The judge tells the jury that they have heard all the evidence and their task is to decide whether, taking it all into account, they judge you guilty or not guilty. 'If you conclude that Mr Tennyson was innocent of the offence as charged, you must return a not guilty verdict. If you agree that there is a suspicion of guilt but the evidence leads you to agree that you have a reasonable doubt about the guilt, then you must acquit the defendant; that is, you must find him not guilty. If you come to the conclusion that Mr Tennyson is responsible for the crime as charged, based on the evidence you have heard, then you will return a verdict of guilty. And you must try and reach a unanimous verdict. It is beholden on me to define the law of the offence charged. The defendant is charged with murder; in British law, that is an offence under common law in which one person kills another with intent to unlawfully cause death or serious harm.'

As he summarizes the evidence, I look at the jury, the men and women who hold your fate in their hands. Has your performance won them over? They have never met Lizzie, but every day here they've been witness to your quiet and steadfast presence, perhaps swayed by your handsome features. Don't we all at some base level expect the beautiful to be morally superior to the unattractive or downright ugly? Wouldn't they all, like I did, welcome you into their family? Bright, charming, talented. Would we be here if your proposal had not been in public? If she'd had more space to consider that proposal? If she'd not been pregnant? If you'd had the lucky break you wanted? A thousand ifs and all their bastard children.

The judge rises and my stomach falls. The jury leave the room.

I am paralysed. Pinned in place until the verdict is through.

And I hope they find you guilty and set me free.

We are called back into the court the following day. The jury has deliberated for seven hours in all, interrupted by an evening break when they were sent to a hotel overnight.

I have not slept.

My stomach is so tense, I fear I will vomit. My mouth waters and I swallow repeatedly. Tony looks as terrified as me. Denise, red-eyed, has been crying.

Bea is holding my hand.

What if they find you not guilty? What then? You'll walk out of here a free man. Will you want vengeance of your own? Want to hurt me, punish me for my avid desire to see you made culpable? It would be so easy. You could take Florence, forbid me to see her. Move away, start afresh. I could not bear that.

The judge begins to speak, asking the foreman if the jury has reached a verdict.

My heart climbs into my throat.

I stare at the woman who is answering the judge, blood rushing in my ears, and the high-pitched whine that never leaves me is accentuated in the brief pause before she gives the verdict.

I squeeze Bea's fingers, watch the foreman's lips. Read the single word.

Guilty.

And it is done.

Ruth

Part Three

CHAPTER ONE

Tuesday 20 July 2010

Except it's not that simple, is it? I thought that with the resolution of Jack's guilt, with the sentence – the judge said he'd serve a minimum of seventeen years – would come a sense of relief, if not exactly closure. Or a feeling of release from the strain of going through the trial in the wake of Lizzie's death. Back then I had regarded his conviction as a goal, a destination on the horizon. Thinking that once I reached that point I would begin to find my feet again. Feel solid ground beneath me: not rock yet, perhaps, but sand or shingle, marsh.

But no. So little has changed. I am still adrift, still drowning in my hate. And guilt.

The hate will be obvious to anyone with half a brain, but the guilt is just as corrosive. A wild, frantic sense of having failed Lizzie, a chill that aches in my guts all the time. The only escape, when my dreams allow, is sleep. Where I forget for long enough and my muscles ease. Many nights I wake with a sense of panic, knowing I will die too, die soon, am dying. Know with a lurch that Florence is dead. Reaching out in bed to feel her warmth, the jump of her heart.

Round and round my mind goes, sifting through the details from the trial, wanting to embrace them, assimilate them, absorb them into every cell and sinew, but how can I do that and achieve peace when so much is still hidden from me? There are too many gaps, holes where his silence, his lies, stain the story.

I wonder if a transcript from the trial would help, but when I enquire, they tell me it would cost over two thousand pounds. Money I don't have. After the cost of the funeral, the money spent on repairing their house (which has now been repossessed), the money I need for Florence, I am living on credit. Something else to worry about.

During daylight hours I have mood swings; anger, bright and fierce and hot, comes from nowhere over the pettiest setback, the most trivial incident.

Stella has turned out to be an idiot. Oozing false sympathy and bitching behind my back in a passive-aggressive way. It would be easier to deal with her if she would be frank, but everything is elliptical and delivered with that blinding smile and indulgent tone.

'Shit-stirrer,' Tony says when I describe it. He takes Florence out, he and Denise; they make a point of stopping for a cup of tea when they bring her back.

Today, in the library, I'm working on lost and damaged: sending out letters to the borrowers whose books are long overdue; assessing items that have been returned ripped or defaced, marked with tea stains or cigarette burns, one with a rasher of bacon used as a bookmark.

Stella hovers over my shoulder. Never a good sign.

'Some people have no respect,' she tuts, nodding at the damaged pile. 'Like animals, some of them. It's a miracle they can read.'

'Most of it's accidental,' I say. 'Though there's a few with malice aforethought, like this one.' I pick up a copy of *Slaughterhouse-Five*. 'Someone has crossed out every swear word in blue biro.'

'It's the ones who scribble *in* swear words that I'm more concerned about,' she says.

'It's vandalism either way,' I point out.

'There's no call for such gratuitous language,' she says.

It's a perennial issue for a small minority of readers, who use our knowledge to help them screen out books they'll be offended by. The majority of borrowers are broad-minded, though, and have no problem at all with earthy prose if it suits the book. The same is true of librarians, who love books with a passion; someone narrow-minded is a rarity in the service. And I'm stuck with her as my supervisor. I think of the Billy Connolly quote: *There is no such thing as bad language. It's just our morals that are fucked.*

'It's not gratuitous. It's a great book, the language fits. Have you read it?'

Stella shakes her head. Does she read? We've not talked books since we met.

'I was going to ask you to unpack and check off the new stock. I hadn't realized this would take you quite so long, though I understand that with everything that's happened . . .'

I push myself up and away from the desk, a sharp pain in my knee as I do. Anger flaring. 'You do it, for fuck's sake, if you think you can do it any quicker. I'll discharge the new stock.'

Her mouth falls open, a perfect circle. I know I should apologize, but I am out of control. I go and hide in the room at the back with the boxes of books that have arrived.

After a couple of days off sick I go back, my tail between my legs. I can't spin it out any longer with Florence to think of now, and although Tony and Denise chip in, I have to earn a living. 'I'm sorry I lost my temper,' I say to Stella. 'I know it's not acceptable. I'm so sorry.'

'Yes,' she says. She's still in a huff, though, her mouth pursed with censure. She punishes me over the next few weeks, on my back all the time, but feigning concern. 'Ruth, have you . . . Ruth, if you're feeling up to it . . . Ruth, could you . . . Ruth . . . Ruth.' Always showing her teeth. Her eyes cold. I dread going into work now because of Stella.

* * *

203

I take Florence to the GP and get a referral for someone who might be able to help her. It means travelling down to London and halfway across the city. A marathon trek, so we stay with Rebecca on an airbed.

The therapist is a middle-aged man, bearded, plump. One of those people whose eyes dance with kindness, so that just seeing him lifts the heart a little. He speaks quite directly to Florence.

The first session, and she is playing with some Duplo dolls on the floor.

'Show me what happened to Mummy,' he says.

Florence stops dead for a minute, and I expect her to withdraw as she so often does, but then she places one doll face down on the floor.

How can she know Lizzie was on the floor like that? Jack said he had shielded her from the scene? *Held her so she wouldn't see.* Did she come down while he was busy setting up his alibi and see Lizzie? Run back up and hide? Did she peep as he carried her out? Or is the way she's placed the doll no more than Florence's interpretation of dead? The doll has to be lying down if it's dead, and she only has two choices of how to put it on the floor.

I don't suppose there are many sentences exchanged over the next hour, but each one elicits a nugget of information.

'What happened to Mummy?' the therapist says.

'She fell down dead,' Florence chants, her chin bobbing up and down on each syllable.

'Why did she do that?'

'Daddy did it.' She knows because I told her after the trial that the court had decided it was Daddy who hurt Mummy and made her dead and he had to stay in prison for a long time.

'On his own?' she said. Was she feeling sorry for him?

'There are other people there – other people who have done naughty things and people looking after them.'

204

She gave one of her inscrutable little sighs and said no more.

The therapist talks to me too, and asks me how I feel about Lizzie's death.

'Furious,' I say. 'I play it over and over. I had hoped with the conviction that it would change.' As I talk, my cheeks flame hot and my belly burns. 'I hate him, I hate him so much. It's not enough, him behind bars.'

'What would be enough?' he says.

I shake my head. There is no reply possible. 'Nothing. Even if I could kill the bastard, it wouldn't bring her back.'

'When I ask you about Lizzie,' he says, 'you talk about Jack.'

'He killed her.'

'You lost her. We all grieve differently; there are recognized stages but we may go through them in different ways, revisit some. You are angry, and if this anger is all-consuming, you may find it hard to reach the other stages. In particular, acceptance.'

How can anyone ever accept this? 'I just want him to pay for what he did, to suffer like I have.'

'There's a saying: "He who would seek revenge should first dig two graves."'

I nod, I've heard it before. 'It is killing me,' I agree.

'Have you heard the term "complicated grief"?'

'No.'

'Grief is a natural process, it's the way we work through and eventually accept the death of a loved one. With complicated bereavement, the process stalls, the bereaved person is stuck, they find it impossible to come to terms with their loss. Unable to move forward.'

I recognize the picture he paints.

'It's more common with unexpected and sudden death. From my contact with Florence, I'd say she may be experiencing complicated grief, and it may be the case for you as well. She will sense your anger and regress further. And the involvement

205

of Florence's father, her other caregiver, in the death is a complicating factor. She is at risk of various negative psychological responses. Guilt for failing to protect her mother, guilt at imagining that her own behaviour led to the attack, that if she had only been really good everything would have been all right. Most disturbingly, an understanding that she is half her mother and half her father. And if he is bad, then half of her is just like him, bad like him.' To save her from such a view, I need to explain that it was Jack's behaviour that was wrong, that was bad, not Jack per se. There are no evil people, only evil deeds.

'For yourself, do you recognize any of these indicators? Do you feel that any apply to you?' He shows me a list headed *Symptoms of Complicated Grief*. I read them. Several resound: excessive bitterness related to the death, excessive and prolonged agitation, the prolonged feeling that life is meaningless.

'I suggest you both need help,' the therapist says.

Florence carries on with him. We have several more excursions to London.

As for me, I have a handful of visits to a bereavement counsellor. Time and again it's the anger I end up talking about, that and the desire for retribution.

CHAPTER TWO

Saturday 13 August 2011

I fantasize about escape. A different life. Perhaps a move away from Manchester. As the months slide by, trapped in the slog of work, the demands of looking after Florence, who is still wetting the bed, still almost mute, and often mutinous, I wonder if we are not paralysed by the impact of Lizzie's murder. Perhaps we are too close to it here, too aware of the gap left by Lizzie. Everything is overshadowed by our loss, everything made piquant, poignant by her absence. Every place, every street, each shop or park or gallery soaked in her memory.

Where would I go? What would I do? How would I make a living? I'm not sure what else I'm equipped to do, and a fifty-nine-year-old woman isn't going to do great in the job market. It would mean finding a way of making money to support us both. A business. Or perhaps some sort of childcare or work as a teaching assistant.

It's Bea who comes up with the idea. She's still in touch with Frank and Jan who had the allotment; they live down in Cornwall and are going travelling over the summer. 'You could stay,' Bea says. 'Jan said it would help to have someone keep an eye on the place.' They have often asked me to visit before but I've never made it. 'You and Florence could have a holiday,' Bea says. 'And it would give you an idea of what it would be like to be somewhere else.'

I get in touch with Jan before I have time to hesitate and we agree that Florence and I will spend four weeks of the summer holidays in their cottage.

I work extra hours and swap shifts to accrue the leave.

The journey is exhausting. We leave at six in the morning and arrive at one. The cottage is a mix of old seaside charm and modern conveniences. Whitewashed stone walls and wooden beams, tiny windows everywhere apart from the large patio doors at the front with a small garden and a view of the sea beyond. Equipped with the Internet and a power shower.

After reading the instructions from Jan and Frank, we walk down the lane to the beach. The air smells so fresh, brine on the breeze, and the water is a dense slate blue, capped with curls of white. The fine shingle scrunches underfoot.

With the instincts of a small child, Florence begins to dig a hole, and I sit down beside her. I feel unsteady, as though I might be blown away. I'm glad the beach is big enough not to feel crowded. The space itself is already overwhelming without hordes of people. When did Florence last get to paddle in the sea? Can she recollect her last trip to the beach with Lizzie and Jack? I've no idea. She was so very young when Lizzie died and I imagine she must have very few concrete memories to cherish. Tony and I have put together a scrapbook for her, photos off Lizzie's computer when we got it back from the police, some of our own snaps, cards and notes.

We wander back when Florence gets thirsty, and after drinks and the last of our sandwiches I make an inventory of supplies. Because Jan and Frank live in the cottage it hasn't got the usual inconveniences of a holiday let. No need to head out for cooking oil or salt or washing-up liquid.

Florence takes Matilda out to the garden while I unpack. The mattress protector is a priority. The village is quite big, spreading up into the farmland behind, but we are near the centre, with its small high street and parade of shops. Half of them are aimed at the holiday set: lilos and buckets and spades hung at the doorways, racks of postcards cluttering the pavement.

We fall into a routine. Woken early by the raucous clamour of seagulls, we have a lazy breakfast then go down to the beach in the morning. Florence plays and I . . . what do I do? I obsess, I suppose. The books I've brought remain unread. I've tried countless times but I still cannot read. No concentration. It's something else Jack has robbed me of. Close to lunchtime, we have a splash-about. The water is freezing, and when we emerge we go home for lunch and to warm up.

It's a lovely place and the sun shines, but it feels unreal. As the week goes on and the second brings rain, I feel more and more uneasy. It takes me a while to realize that I'm homesick. Fish out of water. This place feels clean and full of space and simple natural things, but it is not me. I miss Manchester, its grime and hustle and cheer, the hubbub of it all. The connections that bind me to the people and places, the buildings, the fond familiarity of its skyline. I feel I have abandoned Lizzie. Maybe it is too soon, is all; the time will come when I can leave the place without a sense of leaving her, of not keeping vigil.

Florence plays with another girl one day. And I wonder if she is healing.

We go home a week early.

Friday 23 September 2011

A notice goes out to all city council workers. Offers of voluntary early retirement and redundancy. Work has become unmanageable; Stella still supervises me, every breath I take.

'I'm thinking of taking voluntary retirement,' I tell Bea.

'Could you manage?' Bea says.

'Not on the pension alone, it's peanuts. But my mortgage is paid off, so I'd just need living costs.'

'Just,' she says drily.

'I could start with lodgers again,' I say. 'That would help.'

She nods. 'Might be good to have the company.'

'Imagine the gossip, though. It's a small world, the acting business. This'll be the house where Jack Tennyson holed up after killing his wife.'

'There must be other people who need short-term lets in Manchester,' Bea says. 'Or you could take someone on for an academic year, a student or postgrad. Someone wanting family life instead of grunge.'

The redundancy pay-off would give me some breathing space, a few months to find some other way of making a living, so I go for it. I'm not the only one to take the offer. Morale is low and people like me who've been in the service for years miss the vision and excitement of those early days. It sometimes feels like death by a thousand cuts. I'm still proud of the service, but I know it could be so much better. How long can it last with resources shrinking and provision undermined?

I can't imagine my future. All I see is day following night and the struggle to keep on, to keep on breathing, to keep on getting up and putting one foot in front of the other.

CHAPTER THREE

17 Brinks Avenue
Manchester
M19 6FX

The allotment has gone to seed. Melissa and Mags have kept up with two of the beds and some sections are covered with old carpet, but the remainder is choked with weeds and spinach that has bolted. I've not come here today to plant or dig, but to sit in the soft sunshine and consider what to do. Across the allotment bees drowse and a robin is busy finding worms.

My thirst for vengeance, my dwelling on you and your crime, my hatred – these things keep the wounds of my grief open. I pick away at them. Scratch, scratch, scratch. The sores have become infected. My wrath and my fixation on hating you, defining you as the murderer and nothing more, leaves Lizzie permanently cast as your murder victim above all else. It leads me nowhere, this raging hatred; it fills my head with you, it pins my eyelids open and forces me to see Lizzie in that lake of blood, Lizzie warding off the first blow, terrorized. I don't want to live the rest of my life thinking of my daughter like that.

How can I forgive you? Do I want to forgive you? Do you deserve it? You won't even admit what you have done. I've been studying accounts of the Truth and Reconciliation Commission in South Africa. So many victims, such a huge abuse of state power. The victims had the opportunity to retell the horrors of apartheid; the abusers were offered amnesty for full disclosure of politically motivated crimes. Very different from the Nuremberg Trials in the wake of World War II. The one punitive, the other attempting to restore justice and heal society.

In South Africa, people felt they achieved the truth to a greater degree than any reconciliation. Some argued that reconciliation should not be an alternative to justice but something that follows on from it. I have my justice, because you are locked up, but I am not reconciled.

So many of the other cases I read about, of forgiveness or reconciliation, are underpinned by faith, Christian faith mainly. 'Forgive them, Father, they know not what they do.' I do not believe in gods or ghosts or fairies. There are some breathtaking examples of bereaved relatives forgiving absolutely, unreservedly, relinquishing the anger and the hatred and letting go of any desire for revenge. I cannot imagine it.

What I can connect with is how these charitable people frame their emotional state before the act of forgiveness. Speaking of the yoke of bitterness, the cancer of hate and the power that the murderer exerts as long as he defines their waking lives.

There's a Sartre quote: *Freedom is what we do with what's been done to us.* I'm not free. I may as well be in that cell with you. My hatred, my anxiety, my rage are the shackles I adorn myself with. The longer I resent you, despise you, rail against you, the longer I suffer. But how else am I to be?

Ruth

CHAPTER FOUR

17 Brinks Avenue
Manchester
M19 6FX

Kay calls with the news that you have confessed. I almost fall over, it's such a shock. There's a flight of elation immediately afterwards, a giddy sensation. I am vindicated.

Only later do I begin to think about it more carefully. Is this a gambit so that you can be released sooner? You have to serve a minimum of seventeen years before you can be considered for parole, and you're just shy of three years in prison. No one is eligible for parole unless they show remorse. So if it is a tactic, it is very forward planning.

I don't care, actually. If you're now admitting your crime, I see an opportunity to get to the truth. That's what people wanted in South Africa and the other countries that emulated them: truth and then reconciliation. And I decide that for Florence, for myself, for Lizzie, I must find a way forward.

So we will start with the truth. You will tell me everything. All I need is to find a mechanism for contact with you.

Tony thinks I am insane to want to communicate with you. He doesn't seem as damaged by Lizzie's death, not as embittered by it. He's heartbroken; a pall of sadness clings to him these days, unshakeable. But he is not livid as I am. Perhaps your betrayal feels greater for me because I saw the fruits of your handiwork and sheltered you for the days that followed.

Kay tries to put me off when I ask her about it. 'Restorative justice can be very helpful for low-level crimes – antisocial behaviour, theft, robbery – but it is not used for a crime of this magnitude.'

'There was a case in America,' I say, 'I saw it on the Internet. A couple who have been able to meet the man who killed their daughter.'

'That's very unusual,' she says, 'and I've never heard of it happening over here.' She agrees to make some enquiries. A couple of weeks later and she's telling me she's not made any progress.

'If Jack was willing,' I say, 'and I was too, how can that be a bad thing?'

'You need a professional to set the whole thing up. And I've not been able to find anyone prepared to work with you.'

'Kay, I'm drowning.'

'I'm sorry, Ruth. I can't help. I don't think it can be done.'

I spend hours hunting people online – psychologists, mediation specialists. I send emails, they come back with apologies, with rejections, *no can do*.

I want the truth, to know exactly what you did to Lizzie, to know precisely how she died, to see your remorse. There is no prospect of forgiveness or even acceptance without that. There are so many questions only you can answer.

Ruth

CHAPTER FIVE

Thursday 25 October 2012

I am cleaning the oven, a job I loathe, which means I leave it too long and then it's even harder to do.

Florence is at the kitchen table, messing with Play-Doh.

At first I think I've misheard. I'm on my knees, head in the oven, trying not to breathe in the fumes.

'Daddy hit Mummy.'

I shuffle back, and turn. 'What?'

'Daddy hit Mummy.' It is the first time that Florence has ever initiated any discussion of the tragedy with me. Though I've been warned that she may well revisit the murder time and again as she grows, needing to refine her understanding as she matures intellectually and emotionally, whenever I bring it up she is silent.

'He did,' I say slowly. 'He did, and Mummy died.'

'Lots of times,' she says.

I have never been specific about the murder; she knows nothing about the poker, about the dozen-odd blows. Or have I? Did I say 'lots' to explain why Lizzie was hurt so badly she wouldn't get better? 'Was it?' I say.

'Sick of it,' Florence says, and she bangs her hand on to the Play-Doh. 'Sick of it!' An echo. An echo of Jack? Or maybe Lizzie?

Getting to my feet, I strip off the rubber gloves but keep my distance. I don't want to crowd her. I stare out of the window;

Milky is perched on the wheelie bin at the end of the garden, washing himself.

'Who said that: sick of it?'

'Daddy. Very cross.'

'Yes,' I say blandly. 'Was he downstairs?'

'One day and another day . . .' She makes a noise in her throat as if she's unsure how to phrase it. 'One day,' she starts again, 'in the bedroom and one in the kitchen and lots of days.'

'Daddy hit Mummy on lots of days?' The fizz of adrenalin whips through me. Tightening everything.

'And then she fell down dead.'

I glance over and she's poking holes in the pink dough with her fingers.

'Did you see Daddy and Mummy have that big fight?'

She shakes her head. 'Stay in your room,' she says sternly.

My eyes water and I blink fast. Have I got it right? Did Jack tell her that? Or did she hear what was unfolding and know she had to stay in her room because the violence was a familiar situation?

'Were you in your room when they had that big fight?'

She rubs her nose. Nods twice. Notices dough on her finger-nails and peers at it.

'Did you hear them have that big fight?'

'Yes.'

'Poor Mummy,' I say. 'You were a good girl, Florence, Mummy loved you and when Daddy got cross you hadn't done anything wrong.'

'I stayed in my room,' she says. Like it's an achievement. *I read my book, I brushed my teeth.*

'You didn't see Mummy?' I have to know. She might have crept down when she heard Jack leave the house, seen Lizzie splayed on the floor, her hair dark with blood. Oh God.

She sighs and presses her sticky nails together. 'I stayed in my room,' she repeats irritably.

216

'Are you sad about Mummy?'

She splays her hands like stars and jabs all her fingers down into the mixture.

'Sometimes, perhaps,' I suggest. 'I'm sad sometimes.'

'She might come back,' Florence says to cheer me up.

'No,' I say, 'she can't.'

She begins to scoop the Play-Doh together; her face falls now.

'Let's have a hug,' I say, moving to her.

She gives a little sigh, as though my request is tiresome, but nevertheless stands on the chair and throws her hands around my neck and squeezes, almost choking me. I wrap my arms around her.

'Piggyback,' she clamours.

'Just a little one.'

There's a stabbing pain at the base of my spine as she hikes herself up on to my back. I do a circuit of the kitchen and one of the front room. Florence swings her legs, her heels bumping against my thighs.

Did Jack know? That she was aware of his brutality? Was it Jack who instructed her to stay in her room, or was it Lizzie, desperate to protect Florence from the sight of another beating?

I'm breathless by the time I set her down again. Aware of the oven, smeared in blackening foam, waiting for my attention.

Monday 15 April 2013

It's a chance article in the *Guardian* that leads me to Dr Meredith Jansen. She has been advising on a restorative justice programme in El Salvador and has written a book about it. She trained as a psychologist, went into the health service and developed a role in trauma counselling. She has also been a mediator. Although I can find references to her on the Internet, I don't know how to contact her, until an announcement on

217

LinkedIn that says she is running a training programme based at University College London.

I write to the university and hear nothing.

I ring UCL but the switchboard have no extension number for her.

Then I get an email.

She warns me that she doesn't think she can help, but she will be in Manchester visiting family in a fortnight's time; perhaps we could meet then and she could find out a little more.

The rest is history. Slow-moving, but gradually progressing towards an agreement brokered by Dr Jansen. She meets with me three times, the same with Jack. I start my letters.

And now I wait with her in the prison, in a special room. Wait for our first face-to-face meeting. Dr Jansen, Meredith, will be present; we have agreed the terms of engagement.

Now that I am here, I want to bolt, to turn on my heel and put as much distance as possible between us. My skin feels cold; a chill steals through my stomach and bowels. My ears sing and hiss.

I am frightened.

There is a knock at the door.

They are bringing him in.

Part Four

You sit on the chair opposite me. Your face is pale, drawn, your eyes ringed with shadow.

For a long time I cannot meet your gaze. I study my hands while Dr Meredith repeats the agreed protocol for the meeting. She will be with us throughout, guiding us.

As she finishes, I raise my eyes to look at you, and you glance away and back, away again. Rub your palms together.

Your discomfort is a balm.

'Is there anything you wish to say now?' Meredith asks me. 'Before Jack begins?'

'No.'

'Jack?' She invites you to start.

'I'm sorry,' you say. 'I am so, so sorry.'

For what? I think. Say it, say it. What you've done. I need it spelled out. I need it in letters ten feet tall, lit in neon. I need it carved in granite. I need it broadcast from the rooftops. I need to hear it.

'Please go on,' Meredith says.

'I killed Lizzie, I took her life, and I am so sorry. I'm sorry I did it, and I'm sorry I lied about it. I loved her so much.' Your voice is small, shaky.

I hold myself rigid, desperate not to collapse, to stay strong enough to hear all I've come to hear, to learn answers to all my questions.

'Ruth, is there anything you want to say?' Meredith asks me.

'Why did you lie?'

You blow out a breath, knuckle your fists together. 'I didn't want to end up here,' you say. 'I didn't want to lose Florence.'

I think of her astride your shoulders, curled in your arms that awful night, clinging to your legs and screaming at the police, leaping at the sight of you at the funeral.

'I was scared,' you add after a pause.

In the silence I can hear Meredith breathing, hear the click as you swallow.

'Why have you confessed now?' I say. And as I speak, I am aware that I'm putting off the moment when I hear the full unvarnished truth, because I am frightened.

You begin to speak. 'It was eating away at me. I got very depressed, it was destroying me. I tried not to think about it but I couldn't stop. It got worse. And, erm . . . I started thinking about . . . suicide. A breakdown of sorts. So . . . erm . . .' You take a deep breath, readying yourself to talk.

Fear rises in me like a tornado, swirling black, devouring me, and I start to my feet. Close to fainting, my head prickling, eyes awash with dancing dots. 'I can't do this, I can't—'

'We'll take a break,' Meredith says. 'You don't have to do anything you don't wish to. We can leave at any time. Let's go next door for a moment.'

We leave you and go through to an adjacent space. My teeth are chattering in my head. I can smell Lizzie's blood; the shock feels fresh, my heart bruised and aching.

'Breathe,' Meredith says. 'Slow, steady. Take your time.'

She does not pressure me, nor rush me.

Should I go? Should I leave and try again another time? Would that be any easier? If I go now, will I ever come back? Ever know?

Oh Lizzie.

'I want to carry on,' I say.

Meredith nods.

222

We go back in.

Your face is wet. Your nose red. You have been weeping.

I am poised, on the tightrope, on the cliff edge, at the high point of the zip wire. 'Tell me,' I say. Plunging, tumbling, vertigo in my head.

'That day,' you clear your throat, 'it had been difficult. We were struggling money-wise, we were having to take a break from the mortgage. We'd been shopping and then there was Lizzie's haircut.' You bite your cheek. I wait. 'We had tea and put Florence to bed. Lizzie put Florence to bed,' you amend. 'I was angry, angry about everything, not having any work, the fact that Lizzie had spent over seventy pounds on her hair, but I hadn't said anything to her yet.'

'Why not?' I interrupt.

You consider for a moment, then say, 'Because I wanted to take it out on her. I wanted to hit her. I was winding up to it. I never saw it like that back then, but the course I've been doing, the anger management, that's what I've learnt. I wanted to hit her.'

It is hard to hear.

'She said she had something to tell me, she hoped I'd be happy.' You shake your head several times. I can see the rise and fall of your chest, as if the words are pulsing to escape. 'She was pregnant.'

You knew. Something flies loose inside me.

'I said she'd have to get rid of it. We could barely feed and clothe Florence, let alone another child. We started arguing. She was saying that I could find some other work, office work, temping or a call centre, that we'd manage. She wouldn't listen to me.'

I know what's coming, can feel the vibrations underfoot, sense it in the way every hair on my body rises.

'Did she shout at you?' I say. The need for the tiniest specific, accurate detail is acute. I want it all pinned down, to the nth degree.

'No, she knew not to shout.'

A pang in my heart.

'You'd hit her before?'

'Yes,' you say simply, your mouth working.

'How many times?'

'I don't know, I'm sorry.'

'How often, then?' I say.

'Three or four times a year.'

I hate you. Why could she never tell me? 'You hit her when she was expecting Florence, and the summer before she died, like Rebecca said?'

'Yes.'

'Did you use a weapon before?'

'Sometimes. Not the poker.' Your voice tight.

'What, then?'

'A wine bottle, her straighteners.'

I groan in sorrow. Start to cry, wipe the tears away fiercely.

'Are you all right to continue?' Dr Meredith says. 'Would you like a break?'

'No, I want to go on.' Go on for Lizzie and for Florence and myself. I'm frozen in grief, entombed in my bitter loss. I need a way to shatter the stasis, smash through the crypt I find myself in.

'She wouldn't listen to me.' You speak softly. 'She kept saying that we'd work something out, that another child would be company for Florence, that she'd go back to work soon after the baby.'

'What did you say?'

'I was shouting: "You stupid bitch, you fucking stupid, selfish bitch."' The words are blows. But I will take them: every consonant, every vowel. '"No way are you having a baby, you hear me, get rid of it."' You jab a finger half-heartedly, a faint echo of that anger.

'Where was she? Was she sitting or standing?' I say.

'She was sitting, on the big sofa. I was standing. Then she got up. She was frightened.'

'Frightened of you? How do you know?'

'She had her eyes down.' You take a tremulous breath. 'She knew I was . . . I was losing it. We both knew. She stood up and she said, "No, I'm not going to do that. I'll leave you if I have to." And I don't . . . I don't remember picking up the poker.'

Sweat springs and cools under my arms and at the back of my neck. A chemical taste on my tongue.

'I must have just grabbed it.' You press a hand to your mouth. My toes are curled rigid, my jaw clamped tight. My insides seething.

'I hit her with it.'

'Where?' I whisper.

'Her shoulder.'

'Did you speak?' I ask.

'I said, "You will, you will. You'll do what I say."'

'What then?'

'She lost her balance, fell towards the stove. But she recovered, stayed up, and then she grabbed me.'

'Your arm?' Those scratches. The skin she clawed from you. The damning evidence.

'Yes.'

'Did she speak?'

'She said, "Please don't, please please don't."' Your voice fractures.

Something collapses in me. *Oh my baby girl. My lovely girl. My beautiful young woman. Oh my daughter.* I close my eyes. I breathe. I look at you. 'Go on.'

'I hit her on the arm, then the head.' You start weeping, your nose reddening, the tears running down your cheeks. 'She fell to her knees.'

'Did she speak?'

'No, not again.'

Never again.

'I don't remember much. I know I kept striking out, and then she was still and there was blood. Everywhere there was blood.' You are gulping, gasping as you talk. 'I couldn't believe it. What I'd done. I didn't want anybody to know. I didn't want to be found out. I wanted to run away. Hide. But there was Florence. I didn't want her to know.'

'All that noise and Florence didn't come down.'

'She knew not to.' I think of Florence's stern instruction: *Stay in your room.* 'I looked in on her before I left and she was asleep.'

'She heard you attack Lizzie,' I say. 'She told me.'

You flinch, cry out. Turn away.

I don't stop. 'And after, you cleared up like they said at the trial?'

'Yes,' you whisper.

'You burnt your trainers?'

'Yes.'

'And sent those texts?' I think of that last message, a fake request to me to babysit. The warm glow when I read it, a moment of connection with Lizzie, and then looking forward to seeing Florence.

'Yes.'

'You left Florence.' Something catches in my throat. 'You left Lizzie and went to the gym?'

'Yes,' you say.

'Your clothes?'

You shuffle in your chair. 'I went the back way, over the playing fields and round behind the shops. Where the takeaways are – there's some dumpsters. I hid them in there, under bags of food waste.'

It is still so astonishing to me, what you have done. I have the facts, but still I cannot comprehend why you killed Lizzie, why you hit her in the first place. So I ask you, 'Why did you ever hit her at all? Did your father hit you?'

226

You blush, a flood of red in your cheeks, up your throat. You swallow. 'No.'

I stare at you. There must be something. 'Jack?'

You inhale sharply, throw back your head. I can see the pulse in your neck. You slowly lower your head to face me. Tears stand in your eyes. 'My mother did.'

Good God. Marian.

'I was a handful, apparently,' you say quietly. Then add more quickly, 'But what happened, it's my fault. There are no excuses. It's down to me.' You hide your face momentarily, then look at me, a naked gaze, anguish in your eyes, a frown across your brow. 'I am so sorry, Ruth. Tell Florence too, please, I am so, so sorry.'

You cannot ask for my forgiveness outright. It is one of our ground rules. There is to be no pressure on me to forgive. No expectation of absolution.

Meredith asks me if there is anything I would like to ask by way of restitution. I shake my head. I cannot imagine what that might be, what would help at all. She asks if I have anything to say before we end, but I don't. Nothing profound or perceptive or acutely intelligent. All I say is, 'Not now. I'll write.'

I am hollowed out.

Exhausted.

EPILOGUE

17 Brinks Avenue
Manchester
M19 6FX

It's taken me a while to write. Months, I know. Things got very difficult again after we met. It was as if I was grieving afresh. It brought it all back. All my energy went into making it through each day and caring for Florence.

If my meeting with you has achieved anything, it is a sort of settling. Lizzie's death was obscene, a horrible tragedy, but now every element of it is known to me, now the ghastly steps of it have been laid out for me in full view, now I have retold it to myself endlessly, rehearsing it, memorizing it until I know every beat off by heart. So the chasm of ignorance that was filled with fantasy has gone. I have the truth. Stark and gruesome and cruel.

I pick my moment to talk to Florence about seeing you. We are at the park, having a picnic of cucumber sandwiches and cheese straws. Near enough to retreat home if she takes it badly.

We sit in the shade of a large oak at the edge of the field. Florence has collected some old acorns, missed by the squirrels, to take home. We will plant them and see if anything grows.

To help Florence I must constantly redraw you as a flawed man but not a monster. As someone who did something terribly

228

wrong but knows it was wrong. Someone who had free will, who is sorry. She needs to know that you accept your guilt and are full of remorse.

'I went to see Daddy, in prison.'

She looks surprised.

'He's really sorry he hurt Mummy, he wishes he hadn't. He wants me to tell you he's really, really sorry. He knows he made everyone sad, that we all miss Mummy, and he's sad about that too. You were good. It's not your fault. You were just a little girl and couldn't help Mummy. What Daddy did was wrong and he is very, very sorry.'

'All her blood came out.'

I swallow. 'Did it?' My heart aches in my chest. 'Did you peep?'

'Yes,' she says.

'I bet that was a bit scary.'

She looks crestfallen. She dips her head. 'Is he coming home?'

'No. You're going to stay with me.'

'For ever?

'Yes, until you grow up and want a house of your own.'

'I don't want a house on my own, I want to stay in your house for ever and ever and ever.'

'Fine.'

Of course I worry about her future. When Florence is eighteen, I'll be seventy-one. What will happen if, or should I say when, my health falters? It is physically hard, the lifting and carrying, running around after her. I thought my child-rearing days were long gone. There will be more emotional challenges too. How could there not be? We will do our best. It's all we can do. That and love.

Her speech is better, she's a little more sociable, a little less clingy now. We no longer make those visits to London, but to be honest, I don't think she will ever truly be free of the impact of your actions. She will have to live with that knowledge and hopefully accept it. Her life will go differently because of Lizzie's murder. It will affect her on the deepest level. To expect her to rise above that, to be unaffected, is unrealistic and unfair. But she will know love and security and happiness with me. I will endeavour to the best of my ability to give her the stability and the reassurance she craves.

Do your parents visit you? I imagine they will, but I don't care much. We have not seen them since that awful time during the trial. Perhaps there wasn't a strong bond there between them and your daughter in the first place, or maybe they decided it was best to stay away. I'm glad: it would have been very difficult for me and an added pressure on Florence, who finds it so hard to trust people.

We're staying put in Manchester. I can't see us anywhere else. A lovely Russian student rents my spare room. I'm looking for work. Most of the time I don't get any response to my applications. I have yet to have an interview. There are so many people competing for so few vacancies. And I have my bus pass now, which is not seen as an advantage by prospective employers. On my CV I have to account for that break in employment, those lost months. I keep changing it from sabbatical to family bereavement and back. I claim all the benefits I can for Florence, but it amounts to a pittance. Like my pension. We live a very frugal life, and Tony contributes. There won't be any foreign holidays or iPhones for Florence.

Slowly, slowly, all those thousands of other memories I have of Lizzie are getting stronger. Gradually replacing that bloody black night of her death. I am winning her back. Reclaiming her. And as I do, the love of her, the joy in her is diluting the bitterness and anger I feel for you. It's fair to say that I no longer crave vengeance, no longer get drunk on imagining your pain, your destruction. I am no longer buried in my grief, no longer on the pyre day and night. It is resolving into something simpler, without the complication of that gnawing lust for vengeance.

I will never forget.

And I know now that it is beyond me to forgive. But having the truth from you has made it possible for me to at least comprehend what you have done. Alien though your actions were, they are no longer unfathomable. Just terribly sad. Such a terrible waste.

I do not know how those other people, the ones who do forgive, reach that point. I do not think you deserve my forgiveness, actually. And I am not sure it is a gift in my power. I think perhaps the only person who can truly forgive you is yourself.

And I will not write again.

Will I ever be able to think of you before it all went so very wrong, as the young actor with promise and talent, a beautiful face, who loved my daughter so, who cared tenderly for his own little daughter? Can you be both that and the killer, the liar? You have to be if Lizzie is to be complete again and not solely your victim.

Dr Jansen asked about restitution. There is one thing that is more important than anything else. That you put Florence's needs ahead of your own. Promise never to seek her out or contact her, never disrupt her life again. You say you love her, and I believe you do. So leave her be. Relinquish her. She can be free of the fear that one day you'll turn up on the doorstep and try to win her back. As can I.

When you took Lizzie, you lost Florence. Accept that.

In addition, I ask this of you – be an example, teach others, however you can. Whatever courses or groups they have in prison, use them to expose your violence, question it, analyse it, challenge it. Show others where it led. Drag it into the public eye, out from behind the sacrament of marriage and the privacy of net curtains and brightly painted front doors. Become an illustration and a force for change.

Do that for Lizzie.

I still have to tread down hard on all the 'ifs' that sprout like weeds in warm rain. If only she had told me. If only you had sought help for your violence. They are poisonous thorns, piercing the soles of my feet.

I am coming through the dislocation of my life. The wound is healing but the scar will remain deep and vivid, extensive and life-changing. I'll never get over what you've done but I will learn to live with it. To live and breathe and love.

Yesterday I called at the library. Stella has gone, moved to the private sector, to make some other minion's life a misery.

I chose a book. I brought it back to the house, and last night I began to read. Just a couple of pages.

It was like coming home. Like I'd found a part of myself again, my humanity.

Farewell.

Ruth